MW00325717

DON'T RUN

(A Taylor Sage FBI Suspense Thriller—Book 3)

Molly Black

Molly Black

Bestselling author Molly Black is author of the MAYA GRAY FBI suspense thriller series, comprising nine books (and counting); of the RYLIE WOLF FBI suspense thriller series, comprising six books (and counting); of the TAYLOR SAGE FBI suspense thriller series, comprising six books (and counting); and of the KATIE WINTER FBI suspense thriller series, comprising nine books (and counting).

An avid reader and lifelong fan of the mystery and thriller genres, Molly loves to hear from you, so please feel free to visit www.mollyblackauthor.com to learn more and stay in touch.

Copyright © 2022 by Molly Black. All rights reserved. Except as permitted under the U.S. Copyright Act of 1976, no part of this publication may be reproduced, distributed or transmitted in any form or by any means, or stored in a database or retrieval system, without the prior permission of the author. This ebook is licensed for your personal enjoyment only. This ebook may not be re-sold or given away to other people. If you would like to share this book with another person, please purchase an additional copy for each recipient. If you're reading this book and did not purchase it, or it was not purchased for your use only, then please return it and purchase your own copy. Thank you for respecting the hard work of this author. This is a work of fiction. Names, characters, businesses, organizations, places, events, and incidents either are the product of the author's imagination or are used fictionally. Any resemblance to actual persons, living or dead, is entirely coincidental. Jacket image Copyright andreiuc88, used under license from Shutterstock.com.
ISBN: 978-1-0943-2399-2

BOOKS BY MOLLY BLACK

MAYA GRAY MYSTERY SERIES
GIRL ONE: MURDER (Book #1)
GIRL TWO: TAKEN (Book #2)
GIRL THREE: TRAPPED (Book #3)
GIRL FOUR: LURED (Book #4)
GIRL FIVE: BOUND (Book #5)
GIRL SIX: FORSAKEN (Book #6)
GIRL SEVEN: CRAVED (Book #7)
GIRL EIGHT: HUNTED (Book #8)
GIRL NINE: GONE (Book #9)

RYLIE WOLF FBI SUSPENSE THRILLER
FOUND YOU (Book #1)
CAUGHT YOU (Book #2)
SEE YOU (Book #3)
WANT YOU (Book #4)
TAKE YOU (Book #5)
DARE YOU (Book #6)

TAYLOR SAGE FBI SUSPENSE THRILLER
DON'T LOOK (Book #1)
DON'T BREATHE (Book #2)
DON'T RUN (Book #3)
DON'T FLINCH (Book #4)
DON'T REMEMBER (Book #5)
DON'T TELL (Book #6)

KATIE WINTER FBI SUSPENSE THRILLER
SAVE ME (Book #1)
REACH ME (Book #2)
HIDE ME (Book #3)
BELIEVE ME (Book #4)
HELP ME (Book #5)
FORGET ME (Book #6)
HOLD ME (Book #7)
PROTECT ME (Book #8)
REMEMBER ME (Book #9)

PROLOGUE

After a decade of failed auditions, it felt good to be in the spotlight, right where she belonged. Olivia took her last bow as the crowd thundered its applause and she reveled in the moment. Another standing ovation—one more than last night. This was her chance to stick it to all the casting directors and producers and agents who had told her she'd amount to nothing.

She wasn't at the Oscars yet, of course, but this late summer Shakespeare theater was no joke. A thousand people, easy, in the crowd, and the venue had sold out night after night. Her lines were ringing now, and when this run ended next week, she knew that a whole new career was ahead of her.

She smiled and bowed one last time as the curtain dropped.

Backstage was hot and crowded, her fellow actors patting her on the back for her performance. She had nailed it tonight. She had almost felt like Juliet, killing herself in the tomb. For a brief, euphoric moment, she had truly felt transported back in time, to another age. That was the beauty of her profession; she got to live a million different lives, ones so different from her own.

"Sorry, Liv," a voice said, "your car canceled."

Olivia looked up to see the stage manager, Mark, a guilty look on his face.

"Seriously?" Olivia said. She frowned. It was late; all the cabs in town would probably be swarmed with students leaving the bars. She could try to call another, but it sounded like more trouble than it was worth.

Looks like I'm walking, she thought to herself with a sigh. But that was okay. Pine Point had been rated as one of the safest small cities in all of Virginia. Most of the crime was small and petty, or came from the college the town was also known for. It wouldn't be Olivia's first time walking home, so she wasn't worried.

Olivia braced herself for the long walk home. It wasn't so bad. It would be refreshing, actually, walking along the boardwalk, along the ocean, with the many others also on their way home. She grabbed her things to go as a crowd tried to get backstage to interview the performers.

But that was when she saw it.

There, in the packed crowd. A pair of eyes. Shining with something... crazed. Too intense. A chill ran up her spine.

They were looking right at her.

"Who's that guy?" she asked Mark, who was pacing around backstage, congratulating everyone.

"What guy?" he asked.

She turned, but he was gone.

Had she imagined it? Maybe she'd gotten too deep into her role, and was now as delusional as poor Juliet could be.

Passing it off as nothing, Olivia grabbed her stuff and headed out the back door. The fresh air hit her in the face, and she took a deep breath, feeling like herself again. Walking shoes on, she began at a fast clip, marching along the boardwalk. There were many groups of people walking around in the more popular, touristy part of the boardwalk. But as Olivia continued down the shore, toward her apartment, the crowds became sparser. She found herself alone, walking under the moonlight.

Waves rolled against the shore, calming her. Above her head, a clear night sky welcomed her. She hugged herself from the cold breeze. Now that it was early September, it was getting extremely cold at night.

She glanced at the barrage of texts on her phone, ignoring them for now—but noticed the time. Almost midnight. She hurried her pace.

And that was when she heard it.

A whistle, behind her. She turned and felt her stomach drop.

The same man. The same crazy, intense eyes.

Fear nearly turned Olivia to stone. But she had to get away. Without a second thought, she ran. She ran so fast she didn't even realize it until she was almost to the end of the boardwalk.

Then, a hand on her shoulder. Olivia screamed and turned. In the shadows, she could barely see him.

"Olivia."

His face, shadowed and sunken in, was not familiar.

"Yes?" she asked, confused. But the man didn't seem immediately threatening. Had she gotten worked up for nothing? "You scared me," Olivia said, trying to act normal.

"I'm sorry," he replied. He was smiling, but his eyes were blank. "What's the rush?" he said.

She didn't answer. She didn't know what to say, but she was slowly backing away. He followed.

"The play was great tonight," he said.

She nodded but felt scared inside. Something was very off with

2

him.

She was trying to think of what to say to get away from him. She thought of reaching for her phone.

"When do you rehearse, again?" he asked.

"We don't," she said, softly.

"What do you mean?"

"We don't rehearse. We don't need to anymore. We just perform."

"Interesting, for a bunch of fakers," he said.

He took a step forward. She felt trapped.

"F-fakers?" she stammered.

"How quickly you forget," he mused.

Something in his voice was familiar. She felt as if she knew him but couldn't quite place it.

"I know you from somewhere," she said, still a little out of breath from her run.

"Oh?" he said. "I'm sure you remember me, don't you, Olivia?"

Every molecule in her body screamed at her to run. Olivia didn't let him finish.

She ran.

His footsteps echoed behind her.

Please, God, she prayed as she ran and ran. *Just let me survive this. Please.*

But a moment later, she felt it. His hand on her shoulder. Shoving her.

The impact hurt her ribs, her face, on the wooden planks.

"Help!" she screamed.

But no one was around.

She reached, with shaking hands, for her phone—but he kicked it away.

And the last thing she saw as she stared up at his gleaming eyes was his hand, holding a red ribbon, coming down straight for her.

CHAPTER ONE

Special Agent Taylor Sage walked down Pelican Beach's sidewalk and braced herself against the unusually cool wind coming off the ocean. She needed answers—and she needed them now. Maybe it was foolish to put so much faith in this tarot reader, but Taylor couldn't stop her feet from bringing her here. She drew closer to Belasco's shop with her heart in her throat.

It had been a week since Taylor had been put on leave from the FBI after the incident with Gabe French and losing her partner. Since her husband had left her. And since the tarot reader had ominously predicted someone from her past might come back—someone who, Taylor hoped, could be Angie. Her sister who had gone missing two decades ago.

Tomorrow was Taylor's first official day back at work, and while during the last week, she hadn't accomplished much in her personal time, she needed more information from Belasco before she went back to the field.

She needed to know who the person "coming back" from her past was.

Ben?

Or is Angie alive?

Taylor walked right into the dark shop with no hesitation, surrounded by the familiar smell of burning incense. Miriam Belasco appeared through the curtains. Her expression was stony, yet wise. Like she knew Taylor had been coming. Belasco had thoughtful, knowing eyes. It had always freaked Taylor out. She felt as if she could see right through her.

"I thought I would see you sooner," Belasco said.

Taylor looked at her, pleading. "Please—I need answers. Tell me the truth. I need to know what you meant about the person from my past coming back. Did you mean my husband? Or my sister?"

Belasco stayed silent, studying her.

"I can't sleep," Taylor said. "I can't focus on my work. I feel like I'm losing my mind. Please, I'll pay you."

A moment of silence. Belasco had done so much for Taylor, and Taylor was wondering if maybe, it was starting to wear on her. She looked tired.

"Mrs. Sage… you know money isn't what I'm after."

"But I *will* pay you."

Belasco let out a long sigh. "Sometimes… it's better not knowing the future. I've seen many people over the years, but no one has come into my shop as much as you."

"I'm sorry if it's excessive," Taylor said. "This isn't easy for me to say, but I'm desperate."

After another moment of hesitation, Belasco nodded. "One more time, Mrs. Sage. Then, I think you should take a break. I worry too many predictions could be bad for you."

"Okay," Taylor agreed, even though she couldn't imagine her life at this point without this shop. Before she moved here, Taylor would have been horrified to know she would one day rely on a fortune teller like this. The old Taylor thought this was all bullshit; but she had become jaded by her time here, jaded by everything that had gone wrong in her life. And Belasco's shop was the only place that made her feel, in a weird way, like she was grounded.

Taylor followed Belasco through the curtain, to the back of the shop.

"Sit down," Belasco said, gesturing to the table where the tarot cards were splayed out.

Taylor did, somewhat shakily. Belasco sat on the other side. Normally, this was when Belasco would start shuffling the cards, but instead she said: "Take my hand. It's rare, but sometimes, I can see things even the cards can't tell me. I'm willing to try it for you, as I can tell you're hurting."

Taylor reached out reluctantly. Belasco's cool palms smoothed over hers as she squinted her eyes in thought.

"Now tell me, why should I help you?" she asked softly.

"Because I need the truth," Taylor said. "I can't go on living like this. I have to find my sister." In that moment, getting information about Angie was even more important than Ben. Over the past week, Taylor had missed her husband—but in truth, she was more preoccupied by a blind hope of Angie being alive than anything else.

Belasco's eyes pinched even tighter, her brows stitching together, almost in pain.

"Do you see something?" Taylor asked, her heart in her throat.

"Your sister will be fine where she is," Belasco said. "She knows how to take care of herself. And there are more pressing issues for you."

5

What? Taylor's mind raced. So this was about Angie?

Taylor shook her head. "Please. I don't understand. What do you mean? Is my sister alive?"

Belasco's eyes opened, as though disenchanted. She pressed a hand to her mouth, as if she wanted to say something but then reconsidered. She backed away from her, shaking her head.

"There's nothing for me to tell you. I'm sorry."

Taylor leaned forward and grabbed Belasco by the arm. It wasn't like her to be so desperate—but this was a two-decade old mystery for her, and it was damn personal. If Angie was still alive, and Belasco knew about it—then Taylor needed answers.

"Tell me!" Taylor said.

Belasco met her eyes calmly and firmly. "I've already told you all I know."

"But those are just words. What do they *mean?*"

Belasco's lips curled into a smile, her eyes twinkling mischievously.

"It means exactly what I said before. Someone from your past will return to you."

"But you said my sister can take care of herself," Taylor pleaded. "What did you mean? Is she alive?"

Belasco's frown returned. "Did I say that? I don't recall…"

Taylor couldn't believe her. Was she messing with her? Making things up for drama? For money? Taylor had grown to trust Belasco, but this display caused anger to pool into her.

"Are you messing with me?" she asked.

"I'm not," Belasco said. "If I said that while in my trance, I'm very sorry to tell you that I don't know the meaning. I'm just a vessel for the message, Mrs. Sage. I don't have all the answers."

Taylor relaxed. Maybe Belasco meant what she said. Still, Taylor's head was reeling.

"Listen to me," Belasco said, suddenly firm. "There are many forces at play in this world, forces you cannot understand as yet. I will say one thing about this sister of yours."

Taylor watched with bated breath, anticipating her answer.

"If you want to know your future," Belasco said, "and if you want to find the truth, you must let her go. No matter how much it hurts you. If you don't, you will never be happy. Obsession is your greatest weakness, Taylor Sage. I'm afraid I can't help you any more today."

Taylor couldn't help but feel offended. She hadn't come here for psychoanalysis; she could do that herself. She knew she could be obsessive, but this was different.

6

"That is all, I'm afraid," Belasco said. "I see nothing more about this sister you mention."

Taylor sulked in the chair, defeated, disappointed. And more than anything, she felt foolish. She didn't want to leave here with no answers.

"What about my husband?" she asked. "Can you see anything about him?"

Belasco seemed as though she wanted Taylor to leave. She shifted uncomfortably. "Visions are… taxing on the body and mind," Belasco said. "Inducing them causes great stress to me."

"I'm sorry," Taylor said. She knew she was being unfair and selfish. "But if you reconsider," she added, "I can pay you double."

Belasco's eyes flashed. Despite everything, and all the free readings she'd given her, Taylor knew she needed the money. The shop was beautiful, but small, and it didn't turn up a huge profit. Most of the time, when Taylor came in, there was nobody here at all.

"I will try once more," Belasco said. "But about your husband. Not your sister."

"I understand," Taylor said.

"Give me your palms."

Once more, Belasco smoothed her palms over Taylor's.

Belasco began shaking as she closed her eyes again. "Your husband, Ben… I see him… but he's distant."

Taylor's heart sank. This didn't sound good.

"But wait," Belasco said. "There's… something else. A child."

"With who? Ben?" Her eyes burned. She prayed Belasco wasn't giving her a vision of Ben with *another woman's* child.

"No, with you," Belasco said.

"What?"

It didn't make sense. Taylor had been told she'd never have children. But she had never shared that information with Belasco. She decided to keep quiet and see where Belasco went with this.

"The path to having a child is difficult," Belasco said. "For you, especially. It is long and painful. It is not for the faint of heart. But you want it. You will try desperately..."

Taylor's heart stopped. She felt as if it would rip her in two.

Belasco took her hand and squeezed it.

"They told you… you will never have one," she said.

Taylor couldn't believe it. If everything else hadn't convinced her that Belasco could truly see things—this did. How could she possibly know that?

"But you will have a child of your own," Belasco said. "I can see it in you."

Hope leapt in Taylor's chest, and she wanted to cry. "How do you know?" Taylor said.

Belasco squeezed her hand. "I see a little girl. Her hair is long and thick. It sticks out in the back. She's a little wild. She doesn't do as she's told. She loves animals. Especially horses."

Taylor smiled softly and closed her eyes, imagining this possibility, this world where she really did have her own little girl.

"She's a firecracker," Belasco said. "She'll be the death of you."

"Please, tell me," Taylor begged. "How can you know this?"

Belasco opened her eyes, finally meeting Taylor's desperate stare. "I'm sorry, Mrs. Sage. This is all I can offer you. Any more, and I may not wake up for hours, perhaps days."

"But—"

Suddenly, Taylor's phone rang in her pocket. She was torn between answering and staying. It was probably work—but it could be Ben. Both were equally important. Frustrated, she took out her phone. It was work. She couldn't miss this.

"I... have to go," Taylor said to Belasco. She felt as if something in her life had come full circle, as if she had been moving toward this place, toward this moment, toward this question since the first time she saw the sign for this shop.

She turned to leave but paused.

"What is it?" Belasco asked.

"Nothing," Taylor said. "Just... thank you for everything. And I'm sorry for being pushy. It won't happen again."

Taylor turned and left through the curtain. Her heart was racing. She felt as if she would burst from the answer that had been revealed. Her phone was still buzzing in her pocket, so she zoomed out of the shop, onto the cool, cloudy day, and answered it.

"Hello?" Taylor said.

"Sage, this is Chief Winchester." Taylor's boss, Steven Winchester, was on the other line. "Where are you right now?"

"I'm near my house, Chief," Taylor said. There was no way she could ever admit to the FBI that she regularly visited a tarot reader. That would be the death of her *career*.

"I'm sending you an address," Winchester said. "Get there now. There's been a murder, and you're on the case. You need to meet me and your new partner there ASAP."

A new partner. Taylor had a bad feeling about this.

CHAPTER TWO

Taylor hurried up to a police-swarmed boardwalk in a small city, Pine Point, about halfway between D.C. and Pelican Beach. Her heart pounded in her throat. Two questions had plagued her mind on the drive up. One: Who was dead? And two: Who on Earth would her new partner be?

It was early morning, and the sun beat down on her. This would mark Taylor's first case without Calvin Scott as her partner. As Taylor drew closer to the crowd of officers, she caught sight of Winchester's broad frame. He spoke to another man, who stood apart from the blue uniforms.

This must be him.

The man was at least six-foot-four, built, and had a short, military-style haircut. Sun-tanned skin and black hair. Even next to a mammoth like Winchester, this guy was huge. Taylor appeared next to them, just as Winchester took notice.

"Sage, there you are," he said, eyes hidden behind his sunglasses. "I'm not sticking around, but I wanted to introduce you to your new partner."

"You're Agent Sage?" the new guy cut in before Taylor could say a word.

"Um, Special Agent Sage," she corrected, a bit put off by his bluntness. "And you are...?"

"Special Agent Wesley." He looked away, the sun trapped in his aviators. She couldn't tell if Wesley was his first or last name—presumably last, but why leave out his first name? That struck her as odd. "Good to meet you," he added, softening Taylor a bit. Despite his rugged appearance, he seemed nice, if not a bit closed off.

"You too," Taylor said.

"Okay, you two," Winchester said, "I gotta jet. I'll let you take the lead." He gently clasped Taylor's shoulder. "This one's not pretty."

With that, Winchester was gone. Taylor gulped, nervous to see what they were working with. She faced Wesley and asked, "What are we dealing with here?"

"See for yourself," Wesley said. He gestured up the boardwalk, where officers were taking photos of the scene.

9

A grim feeling rose in Taylor as she approached the scene. Between the officers, she made out the unmistakable shape of a body on the boardwalk. No blood was in sight. As she got closer, she saw it was a pretty young woman, no older than twenty-five. She wore extravagant makeup on her pale, clean face, but she had been positioned so perfectly, so straight, that she looked more like an embalmed corpse in a casket.

But that wasn't the most chilling part.

Her hands had been positioned to hold a single white flower over her chest.

Taylor got a closer look. The petals were strange and curved—Taylor was no botanist, but if she remembered correctly, it was a ghost orchid. She only knew because her mother had painted one before. It was an incredibly rare flower.

"Who is she?" Taylor asked. On immediate inspection, she couldn't tell the manner of death.

Wesley appeared beside her, hands on his hips. "A local small-time actress, apparently. Olivia Newman. She was performing at a theater last night. Some fancy play or something alone those lines."

Taylor turned back to the body. She needed to identify how she was killed, so she knelt in and got a closer look. No stab wounds, no visible blood.

On her neck was a thick red mark.

A strangulation.

But with what?

Judging by the uniform shape of the mark, it hadn't been done with a rope, or hands. It was something else.

Taylor leaned in closer.

Maybe a ribbon?

She stood up and sighed. Taylor looked out at the ocean, where frothy waves rolled in. It was a beautiful spot. Pine Point had a modest population, but it was a college town, meaning lots of new faces appeared—and disappeared—each year. And with the beginning of September, that meant classes were back in. She wondered if it could be related.

Belasco's words from earlier slipped back into her mind, uninvited. Taylor imagined that if she did have a little girl, this would be one of the worst ways to lose her. She felt for Olivia's parents, wherever they were.

Taylor faced Wesley. "What was she doing down here?"

"Guess we're here to figure that out," Wesley said. It seemed like he was being a bit short with her. Taylor's opinion of him slowly soured, but she tried not to take it personally; maybe this was just his personality.

Still, Wesley was a far cry from the friendly, encouraging Calvin Scott. Taylor hadn't expected to miss him so much.

Taylor refocused on the body. Her heart sank. She had seen enough crime scenes to know this was bad. Whoever did this couldn't be left to roam the streets. The position of the flower concerned her even more, as in her experience, tokens were a hallmark sign of someone who had every intention of killing again.

"One of the officers recognized her," said Wesley suddenly. "Apparently, they went to high school together."

Taylor nodded. So, this girl—Olivia Newman—grew up here. Judging by her attire and makeup, Taylor guessed she had been walking home alone late at night when somebody attacked her. Could it have been a crime of opportunity? She wasn't sure; the flower, the ribbon as the potential murder weapon—it was all too deliberate. Almost personal.

Maybe this was even a stalker situation. If Olivia had a bit of a high profile in town, that wasn't unreasonable.

Taylor looked up at Wesley. Unlike her previous partner, he had some age on her, maybe a few years her senior, thirty-eight or thirty-nine. He also seemed a bit tense, and she wondered if he was the talkative type. Doubtful, but she decided to take a chance—she wanted to gauge his attention to detail, see if his theories aligned with hers.

"What do you see?" she asked him.

"Well," Wesley said, "the staging feels pretty deliberate for this to have been random. Considering Olivia had a history in town, and was a local celebrity, I wouldn't rule out a stalker."

Taylor nodded, impressed. Wesley had a keen eye. She looked down the boardwalk again. This was the last place she would expect someone to be murdered. Taylor ran through it all again in her mind.

"He came prepared," Taylor concluded. "I can't say for sure what she was strangled with, but it looks like it could've been a ribbon. Which would line up with the flower." She paused. "It seems he was going for some type of 'beauty.' Perhaps rarity. Ghost orchids are rare, after all."

Wesley looked at her. "You could identify the flower?"

Taylor nodded. "My mom's a painter, and let's just say she likes plants."

Taylor combed the area, trying to look for anything—a hair, a fiber, anything. Her eyes took everything in, but the killer had been meticulous. This was a crime of passion. Maybe even "art." Taylor needed forensics to come in and do a sweep before she could come up with more definitive answers.

Taylor faced Wesley. "Okay, we should—"

"Let forensics do their jobs," Wesley finished for her. "We should talk to the officer who knew the victim again."

Taylor couldn't help her sudden flush of annoyance. Calvin never would have cut her off. It wasn't a seniority thing, either. Her first partner—Jenkins, who she'd worked with for years in Portland—had been old enough to be her father, and he always let her finish. She didn't mind letting experience take the lead, but she barely knew Wesley. Some mutual respect would go a long way when it came to getting in Taylor's good books. But she was here now. She'd been shipped out to Pine Point, and she'd have to make the best of it— especially if a killer was on the loose.

But she wasn't sure how she felt about her new partner. Wesley didn't seem to be the kind of man who would take any lip from anyone, which could be a good thing in the field. On the other hand, he was difficult to read so far. For once, she felt like the roles had been reversed; she remembered how little she'd been willing to let Calvin Scott into her life, and how she herself could be hard to read. Taylor had a feeling that Wesley would sense that, too.

"Okay," she agreed anyway, because that would have been her next move too.

Wesley led Taylor toward a police cruiser, where a young officer in uniform leaned against the hood of his car, looking torn up. When he noticed the agents approached, he stood at attention.

"Oh, it's you again," he said to Wesley. "Did you find anything out?"

"Officer James," Wesley said, "this is my partner, Special Agent Taylor Sage."

Taylor extended a hand, and James shook it. "Good to meet you," Taylor said, "and I'm sorry for your loss. Special Agent Wesley informed me that you knew the victim."

"Well, sort of," James said. "We went to high school together, but we weren't close."

"Can you tell us anything about Olivia that might help us understand why this happened to her?" Taylor asked.

"Honestly, I have no clue," James said. "I do know that Liv's parents live across the country, and she grew up here with her grandma, who died at the end of high school. Last I heard, she was still living with her best friend Frankie. Frankie and I sort of had a thing, and I've been to their place a couple times."

"So Frankie is her roommate," Taylor clarified. "We—"

"We're gonna need that address," Wesley cut in. Taylor gave him a look, but he didn't seem to notice. "Any chance you can get that for us, James?"

James nodded and pulled a notepad from his uniform's pocket and scribbled something down, then handed the paper to Wesley.

Taylor side-eyed him. But she didn't have to get along with her partner in order for this to work—she just needed results.

CHAPTER THREE

Taylor braced herself as she knocked on the door to Olivia's apartment. It was a rental unit above a Chinese food restaurant, not the most expensive-looking place. But making a living as an actor in a town like this must have been hard for Olivia—before she was murdered.

Wesley was silently at Taylor's side. He hadn't said more than a few words since they'd gotten out of their cars and made their way up to Olivia's apartment to talk to her roommate. As far as partners went, Wesley wasn't leaving a great first impression. He was standoffish, and Taylor couldn't help but get the sense that he didn't have confidence in her abilities as an FBI agent.

After a few moments, a girl in her early twenties, wearing oversized Tweety Bird pajamas, answered the door. Mascara ran down her face, and she blew her nose into a Kleenex as she gawked at the agents.

Clearly, she had already been notified of her roommate's murder.

"Oh, God," she said, "this is about Olivia, isn't it?"

Taylor nodded. "Hi. Are you Frankie, Olivia's roommate?"

"Yes, oh my God," Frankie said. "I can't believe it. Are you two cops?"

Taylor opened her mouth to speak, but Wesley cut her off.

"We're with the FBI," he said. "We were hoping to ask you a few questions about your roommate."

"Oh my God," Frankie said, throwing her hand over her mouth. "Olivia. She's dead. Oh my God."

"Frankie, is there somewhere we can sit down and talk?" Taylor asked.

Frankie nodded, wiping her eyes clear. "Yeah. Sure. I can't believe this. This is crazy."

Taylor and Wesley trailed after her into the living room of the apartment. It was small and cramped. There were two tiny, beat-up sofas, a bookshelf with a large TV, and a coffee table that had been worn down in the middle of the center island. Taylor had been in hundreds of places just like this. The small living quarters in the college city. The crowded streets. The young adults doing their best to make it in a competitive world.

Taylor used to be one of them. And now she was here, working as a bona fide FBI agent. It was a long way from TV dinners.

Frankie sat down on one of the sofas, and Taylor sat down on the edge of the other. Wesley stayed standing, which Taylor found rude.

"I'm so sorry," Frankie said, sighing. "I'm just so shocked. I can't believe she's really gone."

"What was the nature of your relationship with Olivia?" Wesley asked, crossing his arms over his chest.

Taylor was taken aback by his abruptness.

"We were roommates," Frankie said. "What do you mean?"

Taylor cut in, "I think what my partner means to say is, how well did you know Olivia?"

"We were best friends," Frankie said. "Since we were kids. Seriously. She's like a sister to me. I still can't believe she's gone..." Frankie shivered and hugged herself, tears still pouring down her face.

"I'm sorry for your loss," Taylor said. Clearly, Wesley wasn't going to contribute to the compassionate side of the conversation. Taylor wasn't used to being the one who needed to speak up about emotions first. But this wasn't the time anyway; she needed to find Olivia's killer. "Can you think of anyone who might have wanted to hurt Olivia?" Taylor asked.

"A jealous ex-boyfriend?" Wesley added.

"Not really," Frankie said. "I mean, she dated a few guys, but none of them seemed crazy. I always sort of worried for her though, you know? I mean, being an actress and all... can't that sometimes attract the wrong kind of attention?"

"It can," Taylor said. "Did Olivia ever talk about any situations where she felt like she was in danger?"

"No," Frankie said. "She didn't tell me anything that was really worrying her. I did just hear her on the phone with some guy though. I think she was auditioning for something. I don't know. I left the room."

"Do you remember anything specific that she said over the phone?" Wesley asked.

"No," Frankie said. "I just remember her being all emotional about something."

"Do you remember who she was talking to?" Taylor asked.

Frankie shook her head. "No, I don't think so. She just said that he was a director or something."

"What about her job?" Wesley prodded. "Was she getting any weird fan mail? Did she have any crazy people following her around?"

"Not that I know of," Frankie replied. "I mean, she was in a few things here and there, but nothing that would cause some kind of crazy stalker. Olivia didn't have a big social media presence either. I think she was more famous in her mind, you know? That's why she got that nose job. She thought it'd make her famous."

Taylor paused, thinking on that. A nose job? That wasn't a cheap procedure.

"Nose jobs are expensive," Taylor said, glancing around the apartment. "How was Olivia able to afford that?"

"She's been saving up since high school. She was just starting out in the acting world. It's hard to make a living right away. But she was getting by with her waitress job until she could get a gig in a movie or something. The theater was starting to pay her an okay wage, though. Every cent Liv had basically went to saving for the nose job anyway. All she wanted was to be pretty and admired, you know? I guess that's every girl's dream."

Taylor looked around the apartment, tuning out of the conversation.

She could see the tiny kitchen through the door. Poor Olivia had worked so hard, saved up tens of thousands of dollars for a procedure, only to die at a young age anyway. It all made Taylor's heart hurt.

Belasco's words returned again. She had shut down on the topic of Angie, but when she was in her trance, Taylor was certain Belasco had said Angie was "fine" where she was. So did that mean she was "fine" being dead and gone—or was she "fine" alive somewhere?

Shaking it from her head, Taylor refocused on the case; she was here to solve another girl's murder, not ruminate on her own troubles.

She glanced around again and caught sight of the kitchen.

Through the door, on the table, was a vase of flowers.

The image immediately struck her. Olivia had been found dead with a ghost orchid on her. Those looked more like regular tulips, but still—the flower detail was significant.

"Frankie," Taylor cut in, "are those your flowers in the kitchen?"

Frankie's head whipped around. "Huh? No, those were Liv's."

"Do you mind if I take a look?" Taylor asked.

"Not at all."

Taylor hurried into the kitchen, her heart pounding, and picked up the vase of flowers. Wesley appeared behind her but said nothing.

Frankie poked her head in the doorway. "She's been getting those delivered here for a few months, actually. Maybe once every other week. I think they're from a secret admirer."

"And you didn't think that was an important detail to mention?"

16

Wesley asked, irked.

Taylor shot him a death glare that he didn't seem to notice. His attitude was unnecessary. Frankie was clearly grieving—it had probably slipped her mind.

Frankie seemed dumbfounded, so Taylor asked, "Do you know anything about the sender?"

"Not at all," Frankie blabbered. "I mean, there was one time I saw a delivery truck drop them off outside, but I can't remember the name. There was a flower symbol on it or something. I'm sorry, I'm not trying to hide things, I just—"

"Everything is fine, Frankie," Taylor said. "You're doing a great job."

Frankie nodded thankfully, and Taylor refocused on the flowers.

"We need to find out where these came from," Taylor said, setting the vase back on the table. She checked around the stems but saw no cards or tags or anything to show where they had come from. She took a photo of the arrangement, then snaked around the table, where they kept a small recycling bin. No sign of any tags. "There weren't any letters with them?" Taylor asked.

"Um…" Frankie trailed off. "I thought I used to see cards on them, but maybe Liv threw them out."

Maybe… or maybe she kept them somewhere else. The fact that Olivia kept the flowers out, instead of throwing them away, told Taylor that she may have liked the attention.

"Frankie," Taylor asked, "do you mind if we take a look around Olivia's room?"

"No need to ask," Frankie said. "You're welcome to anything here."

She led them back to Olivia's room and let them in. Taylor looked around; it was much messier than she'd expected. There were two desks; one was obviously a vanity, with foundation and makeup brushes, and the other was a workspace, with a few sheets of paper scattered about.

"Did Olivia use this desk?" Taylor asked.

"Yeah," Frankie replied. "She was on it a lot. Like I said, she was saving up for a nose job, and she was trying to make a go of her career in film. She mostly just scored jobs in plays, though."

"What kind of plays?" Wesley asked.

"Theater and opera," Frankie said. "A few parts in films. Nothing major. She had to pay rent, you know? She was a stage actress, and she was great at it. She never got the chance to play a big role in a movie, but she had a whole slew of small roles. She did a lot of background work for movies and TV shows too."

"Wesley," Taylor said, "why don't you check out the desk and see if you can find any notes? I'm going to see if there's a computer we could check."

Wesley nodded and took the desk chair. Taylor scoured the room for a computer, maybe a laptop tucked under the bed...

But what she found made her heart pick up.

There were several greeting cards tucked under the bed. Taylor picked one up. They were all the same. They read: Gloria's Flowers.

Standing, Taylor flashed it at Wesley, whose expression was emotionless.

"Guess we know where the flowers came from," Taylor said.

"Yeah," he said in a dry voice.

Frankie poked over, and her eyebrows shot into her forehead. "That looks just like the symbol I saw on the delivery truck!"

Taylor looked down at the ornate, sparkly writing on the card. "I think we should pay them a visit."

CHAPTER FOUR

The smell of fragrance assaulted Taylor's nose when she walked into Gloria's Flowers. Bouquets were set up everywhere. Taylor had a hard time believing a killer could have shopped here—or maybe, he even worked here.

Wesley came in after her. Against the floral backdrop of the store, he looked completely out of place. The man was rugged and stern. Taylor was having a hard time figuring out how she felt about her new partner—mostly because they had hardly spoken a word to each other, having driven to each spot in their own cars.

He was a bit rough around the edges for her liking; Taylor had always appreciated a direct, but soft approach when it came to interviewing friends, witnesses, etcetera. But Wesley's style seemed to be harsh and to the point. Whether or not that made him a good FBI agent was yet for her to discover.

A teenage, acne-faced employee came up to them and asked, "Hi there, can I help you?"

His face went pale when Taylor and Wesley both flashed their FBI badges.

"Whoa, what's going on?" the employee asked. His nametag read Adrian.

"Hi, Adrian," Taylor said. "We were hoping we could ask you a few questions about a series of deliveries that have come from this shop."

"Oh, sure!" Adrian said. "How can I help?"

"Do you recognize this address?" Taylor handed him a paper with Olivia's address on it.

"No, I can't say I do," he said.

"Flowers from this store have been delivered to it," Wesley said, his voice deep and gruff as if he was going to cuff the kid.

"Uh—I'd have to look that up," Adrian said. "Maybe I should get my boss. Follow me."

They went over to the back of the shop, behind the counter. Adrian shouted, "Merle, are you around?"

A tall, overweight man waddled out from the back of the store. He had thinning brown hair and stubble lining his jaw. Despite his homely appearance, he had warm eyes and wore a colorful uniform made up of blue pants and a shirt with a flower embroidered on it.

"How can I help you folks?" he asked.

When Taylor and Wesley showed their badges again, Merle's expression turned concerned.

"We're looking into a series of deliveries that came from this shop," Taylor said and showed the paper with Olivia's address. "Do you recognize this address?"

Merle frowned at the paper, before he turned his attention to the computer that was on the cash counter. "Let me take a look." After clacking away at the keyboard, his frown deepened. "That's odd. Are you sure it came from this store?"

"Is there another Gloria's Flowers in town?" Wesley quipped.

"No," Merle said, "we're it. Well, I can tell you folks that we've never delivered to that address before. Not on record, anyway."

"We have an eyewitness who claims she saw your delivery truck drop them off."

"Are you sure? I really don't see the address in our records."

Taylor stood back and crossed her arms, considering the possibilities. Those flowers had definitely come from here. The cards were undeniable proof. Taylor would consider the idea of an anonymous customer dropping them off—if Frankie hadn't seen the delivery truck drop them off.

This could only mean someone was delivering them off the books.

"Do you mind if we speak to a few more of your employees?" Taylor asked.

"Go right ahead," Merle said. He gestured to a woman across the room. "That's Tiffany. She might be able to help out."

Taylor and Wesley went over as Tiffany was sorting roses into an extravagant display.

"Tiffany?" Taylor asked.

Tiffany jumped, dropping a rose into the vase. She turned around and gave the agents a smile.

"Hi, I'm Special Agent Taylor Sage, and this is my partner, Special Agent Wesley," Taylor said, noting that she still didn't have her partner's full name. "We're with the FBI."

Tiffany turned around, her long blonde hair pulled back in a ponytail and her blue eyes wide. She was pretty, with a great figure, but Taylor had a feeling that wasn't what got her hired.

"We're investigating a series of flower deliveries," Taylor said. "We were hoping you might be able to help us."

"What's going on?" she asked, concern crossing her light features.

20

Taylor showed her the paper with Olivia's address on it. "Do you remember a delivery from this shop to that address?"

Tiffany thought for a moment before shaking her head. "Not off the top of my head. But I could easily check the computer records to see if we have a record. I'm sure I have the address programmed in there somewhere."

"I don't think you need to waste your time," Merle said, cutting in. Taylor hadn't realized he'd come over as well. "I can tell you with absolute certainty that we've never delivered to that address before. I already checked. And I just checked again."

"How can I help, then?" Tiffany asked, her voice innocent.

"Have any of your coworkers ever made any deliveries off the record?" Taylor asked. It was a longshot, but if anyone had ever acted odd, then Tiffany might be able to help. Taylor was certain that whoever murdered Olivia—and delivered those flowers—was, at the very least, male. A female wouldn't fit the profile, in this case.

"Not that I know of," Tiffany said.

"Any of your coworkers ever rub you the wrong way?" Wesley asked. He glanced at Merle, then Adrian, who was still across the store, pretending to be busy—but clearly still listening.

Taylor wasn't sure Wesley's abrupt approach was the best. Even if Tiffany had been rubbed the wrong way, the only other two men in the store were right there.

"Of course not!" Tiffany exclaimed. "Gloria was my grandmother. Merle is my stepdad. We're all family here, more or less."

Taylor searched Tiffany's face for any sign of anxiety or nerves, but she saw nothing. It seemed she was being honest.

This was leading nowhere fast. As Taylor glanced around at the sea of flowers surrounding her, she was looking for one in particular. A ghost orchid. She didn't see one—but that didn't mean one had never been here.

"One more question," Taylor said. "For you too, Merle."

Taylor took out her phone and the picture of the ghost orchid she had received from forensics. Its curved petals were pure white.

"Do either of you recognize this flower?" Taylor asked.

Merle's brows pinched as he observed, and Tiffany peeked over to get a closer look. Tiffany shook her head.

"I don't know, sorry... flowers are in the family business, but I'm honestly not an expert."

"It's a ghost orchid," Merle cut in. "I've seen it before."

"Here?" Taylor asked. Her pulse jumped.

"Not a chance." Merle almost laughed. "It's incredibly rare, and we tend to focus more on the commercial types of flowers. You know, tulips, roses..."

The contents of the store definitely backed up his claim. Taylor didn't see many unique bouquets. They were all pretty, but generic.

So, they had no record of the delivery, but it had definitely come from here. Neither Adrian, Merle, nor Tiffany seemed particularly sketchy in terms of their demeanors. That didn't mean they were innocent. However, Taylor had a gut feeling there was more at play here. The flowers had definitely come from this store.

A sudden thought struck her.

If an employee hadn't delivered the flowers—what about the delivery driver?

"Do you have a delivery driver?" Taylor asked, turning her attention to Merle.

"We sure do," he said. "New guy, actually. Pretty young. But he's a good kid. He wouldn't steal from the shop."

"Could he not have bought the flowers and delivered them in secret?" Wesley cut in.

"Well, I can't say for sure," Merle said. "Why don't I give you his address? He's off today, but you can go talk to him yourself. I'm sure all this can get sorted out."

"Please," Taylor said.

Merle wrote down the address and phone number on a piece of paper, then handed it to Taylor. "But he's just a kid, really. I don't think he'd do something like that."

The guy's name was Chris Davy. Taylor looked up at Wesley, then nodded at Merle.

"Don't call Davy, Merle," Taylor said. "He's now a murder suspect."

CHAPTER FIVE

Taylor and Wesley approached Chris Davy's house, and Taylor took note of the small Ford sedan parked in the driveway. Apparently, Chris had just dropped out of college and was now delivering for Gloria's full-time. Whether or not he killed Olivia was yet to be determined.

The house looked normal enough: single-story, semi-detached, with flowers blooming in the garden. They reached the front porch, and Wesley went to knock, but Taylor stopped him—she didn't want to go into this thing blind, with a partner she'd barely known for five minutes. A partner who seemed extremely uncooperative thus far.

"Hey, Wesley, hold on," Taylor said. "We should go over our approach. Together. You know, make a plan."

Wesley faced her and took off his sunglasses. He looked down at her with eyes so gray, they were almost silver. The sunlight made them shine like metal. Taylor had gray eyes too—but hers had more of blue in them. But she saw no color on Wesley at all.

There was something intimidating about him, and Taylor didn't like feeling this way. Especially after working with Calvin as her partner, she was used to being in charge, but Wesley was a bit of a loose cannon—he clearly had his way of doing things, and so far, it seemed like he felt Taylor was more of an afterthought. The spark of teamwork wasn't there yet.

"What's there to go over?" Wesley asked. "We talk to the guy, scare him a bit, see how he reacts, and if he refuses to talk, we tell him he's coming down to Quantico with us if he doesn't cooperate."

Taylor paused, considering what he said. "Maybe we should be a bit gentler than that," she suggested. "Prod him a bit, gauge his reactions."

"That's not really how I do things."

"But it is how I do things," Taylor retorted. She was starting to feel seriously annoyed with him. "I know we've just met, but we're meant to be partners, Special Agent Wesley—I'd appreciate it if we could try to stay on the same page."

The air grew thick with hostility, and for a moment, Taylor regretted opening her mouth. But she had to stick to her guns. Being a relatively small woman in the FBI, especially, required her to be assertive, and Wesley wasn't the first alpha male she'd had to deal with in her career. He certainly wouldn't be the last, either.

But he wasn't replying. A total brick wall. Great.

Frustrated, Taylor knocked on Chris's door. They would just have to wing it and figure it out. Moments later, a skinny, buck-toothed kid—early twenties—opened the door.

"Can I help you?" he asked, his voice reedy.

"Are you Chris Davy?" Taylor asked.

"Yeah…"

"We're with the FBI, I'm Special Agent Taylor Sage and this is Special Agent Wesley."

"Wait, what?" Chris looked from Taylor to Wesley and back again. "You're kidding, right?"

"We need to ask you a few questions," Wesley said.

"I don't understand," Chris said, shaking his head. He was clearly nervous, beads of sweat forming on his brow. "Did I do something wrong? I mean, I know I'm going to dread my mother's reaction to this…"

Everything about Chris screamed that he was nervous. Taylor couldn't help but feel suspicious. "No, no, we're not here to arrest you," she said. "We're investigating a murder, and we were hoping to talk to you."

Behind Chris, the house was dark and smelled of air freshener. The walls were bare, and Taylor guessed that it was furnished by the generic furniture store down the street.

"Uh, okay, um, come in?" Chris stammered.

Taylor and Wesley entered the house without hesitation.

"Please take your shoes off," Chris said. "I don't like dirt in the house."

"I think I'll keep mine on," Wesley said.

Chris's face twitched. "Uh, no, can you take them off please?"

Taylor's brows raised in surprised. She hadn't expected someone of Chris's stature to act aggressively—especially against a giant like Wesley.

Wesley's face twitched. Taylor didn't appreciate Chris's attitude either—but she wanted to get more information out of him before going full force, so she politely took off her shoes. It was not a big deal.

But Wesley didn't budge. "The shoes stay on," he said.

Chris twitched more. "You can't come in if you don't take them off."

Taylor gave Wesley a look, hoping he'd take the hint. She didn't want to provoke Chris. Wesley didn't seem to care at all.

But Taylor couldn't force the shoes off Wesley's feet, and neither could Chris. Chris, though agitated, seemed to give up, because he said, "Just—come in. Be careful."

They followed him into the living room, which was unusually bare for a young guy. Only a TV was set up with a gaming system hooked up to it, opposite a couch. Both Taylor and Wesley remained standing, as Chris didn't offer them a seat.

"W-who died?" Chris asked.

Taylor wasn't sure if she wanted to drop a name—not yet. If Chris really was their guy, then he already knew it was Olivia Newman who died.

Maybe he was the one who killed her.

"Nice place you have here," Taylor said, gesturing around the room with her hand. "You could fit a lot more stuff."

"I like clean spaces," Chris said, eyeing Wesley's shoes. Taylor couldn't help but think that if Wesley just removed the damn shoes, this could go a lot smoother. She decided to take the reigns and kept her voice calm, while still keeping the interrogation alive. Chris was definitely suspicious.

"It's a bit empty, though," Taylor said. "Is that just how you like it?"

Chris's voice grew defensive. "Yeah, what's wrong with that? I'm not allowed to like my own things how I want them? It's not like anyone's ever over here anyway."

"Ah," Taylor said. "So you don't have many friends."

"N-no, I mean, I have friends," Chris stuttered.

"But they don't come around that often, do they?"

Chris paused. He glanced at Wesley, like he was trying to get him to approve of something he wanted to say. After a moment, though, he just said it. "The truth is, I don't have any friends. I guess I just don't get along with people well."

"That why you dropped out of college?" Wesley said.

"No, I dropped out because it was bullshit," Chris said.

"And you just got your job at Gloria's," Taylor said. "Surely you've made a few friends there."

"Yeah, but that's not like a friend," Chris said. "I mean, that's just someone who hires you to do a job. I don't have friends in the sense you're thinking. Friends make messes."

Taylor noticed that Chris's pupils were dilated. Definitely on something. "Do you do drugs, Chris?"

25

"Of course not," Chris said, looking offended. "I just smoke weed sometimes to relax. It helps with my ADHD."

"I think it's time we cut the shit," Wesley muttered.

Taylor thought so too. She took a deep breath and said, "Chris, do you know of a local actress named Olivia Newman?"

Chris began sweating and shaking. "Uh, no?"

Wesley took a step closer to him. "Are you sure about that, Chris?"

But Chris looked up at him, offended he was so close. "Hey, back off, man." He looked at Wesley's feet. "And when was the last time you washed your shoes? Honestly, I think you two should go."

"Answer the question," Wesley uttered.

Animosity quickly rose in the room. Chris scowled up at Wesley— before his gangly arms flew forward in an attempt to shove him.

Wesley barely moved. Chris was stick-thin. He didn't have a chance of beating him in a fight. Wesley, on the other hand—he was a mountain.

Still, Wesley's eyes widened at the gesture, and it seemed Chris was so shocked by what he'd done, he didn't know what to say. "I-I'm sorry," he stammered. "I'm sorry, I didn't mean to."

Wesley had a look of rage on his face, and Taylor was thankful he didn't draw his gun. She knew she had to defuse the situation. With startling quickness, she darted in between them and threw her arms between the two men.

"It's okay, it's okay, we're just talking here," she said.

Chris looked at her, still upset, as if he were asking why she was colluding with him and not Wesley. *Maybe if Wesley had taken off the damn shoes,* Taylor thought, *this wouldn't be happening...*

Wesley was little calmer, but he was still angry. "Funny, Chris, that you're defending yourself so hard. I mean, isn't that a bit excessive for someone who's innocent?"

"Innocent about what?" Chris demanded.

"You know what," Wesley said. "You killed Olivia Newman."

"No, I didn't! How dare you say that?" Chris shoved past Taylor and threw his arms at Wesley again.

This time, Wesley twisted Chris around with ease. Chris winced in pain as Wesley snapped cuffs on his wrist.

"Chris Davy, you're under arrest for assaulting a federal agent," he said, then began reading him his rights.

Taylor let out a long sigh, hands on her hips. If not for the high testosterone in the air, that could have gone way better. Although she'd had her fair share of perps lose it on her in the past, so she didn't fully blame Wesley for this. She blamed Chris. Still, Wesley's lack of cooperation with her was leaving a pretty big stain on their partnership.

"Wesley, keep him here," Taylor said. "Let me take a look around."

"No, don't!" Chris shouted.

"Quiet, shitbag," Wesley demanded, holding Chris's cuffed arms behind his back. He then nodded at Taylor. "Go ahead, Sage."

Taylor crept down the hallway. Everything was immaculately clean—the bathroom reeked of bleach as she walked past it, and the hardwood floor was still shining from the polish. She thought back to the way Olivia's body had been found. It was all so clean, so precisely staged. Not a hair on Olivia's head was misplaced.

So far, Chris could fit the profile. But Taylor had no proof he even knew who Olivia was.

Until she stepped into his bedroom.

And on his wall, beside his bed, was a myriad of photos of Olivia Newman.

Olivia up on stage.

Olivia leaving her apartment.

Olivia's selfies from her social media.

Olivia through the window of a coffee shop.

It was a full-blown stalker wall—a shrine.

CHAPTER SIX

In the interrogation room at Quantico, Chris Davy sat across from Taylor and Wesley as they interviewed him. Taylor had seen the shrine to Olivia—he had clearly been stalking her and was the one who had been sending her flowers. Her "secret admirer." But was Chris really the one who killed her?

Neither Taylor nor Wesley took the lead; they both had equal footing. Taylor was softer, more practical, while Wesley had a more direct and aggressive approach. But it was working to get Chris talking, so Taylor didn't mind sharing the spotlight. Still, the dynamic between her and Wesley already felt so different from how natural things had been with Calvin.

"How long have you been stalking Olivia Newman, Chris?" Taylor asked.

"I wasn't stalking her," Chris replied, offended. "I was just—I was just admiring her, okay? She's really beautiful."

"Yeah, we know." Wesley scoffed. "But she didn't feel the same way about you, did she? Did she even know you existed?"

"No, but—" Chris blabbered, his face red. "She's different."

"We know you sent her flowers, Chris," Taylor cut in. "How long had you been stalking her?"

"I wasn't! I never hurt anybody, okay? Maybe we hadn't met yet, but—we were going to. She's different. She's not like other girls," Chris said.

"You're right, Chris," Wesley said. "She's not like other girls. She's dead. And you killed her."

Chris shook his head, eyes pleading and desperate. "No, I didn't kill her. I would never hurt her!"

"But you sent her flowers, Chris," Taylor said softly. "How did you even know who she was? Where did you meet?"

Confusion cluttered Chris's face. "I didn't meet her. I just... I just sent her flowers. I've been watching her, and I know she's the one I want to be with. I've been waiting to meet her."

"Then you know she was killed," Taylor said. "And you know you're a suspect."

"But I didn't do it!" Chris cried. "I just wanted to meet her, that's all.

28

I didn't need to—to kill her."

"Who did, Chris?" Wesley pressed, leaning in. "Who else would have done it?"

"I don't know!" Chris said. "But I didn't do it! I never met her, I just wanted to talk to her!"

"How can we believe you?" Taylor asked. "You have pictures of her all over your room. Your obsession clearly got out of hand. Did you get desperate when she wouldn't return your advances?"

"I'm not obsessed with her," Chris said. "I know that she's beautiful and I respect that, but I recognize beauty in something, and it's not the same as obsessing. I'm not obsessed with anything."

Except for a meticulously high level of cleanliness, Taylor thought, thinking about Chris's immaculate apartment.

This was going nowhere, and Taylor considered an alternative approach. Something gentler, to prod him rather than scare him. Something to get into his head and get him talking.

"But you clearly care about her a lot," Taylor said. "And if she was really your friend, you would help us figure out who really killed her. That's what friends do, Chris."

"I… I don't know," Chris said.

Wesley glanced at Taylor, as if telling her that it was time to step it up get another notch. They'd been talking to Chris for long enough and had received nothing but useless denials. But there was one question that would absolutely answer whether Chris was the killer or not:

"Where were you last night, Chris?" Taylor asked. "Olivia had a show in town. Were you there?"

"I couldn't make it," Chris said. Suddenly, he had a look of hope on his face. "I can prove I'm innocent. I have an alibi for last night!"

"Yeah, and what's that?" Wesley remarked sarcastically.

"I was forced into a family dinner," Chris said. "I wasn't even in town. Call my mom and ask her. I was gone all night. I didn't get back until noon today. That's why I took a day off at the flower shop."

Taylor paused and gave Chris a look. If that were true—then that would clear Chris of the murder.

"Your mom will verify you were there?" Taylor asked.

Chris nodded exuberantly, like a child. "Yes. Absolutely. I didn't even know Olivia died until this morning; I swear. I just found out when you told me. I didn't know she was gone..."

"Okay, Chris," Taylor said, standing up. "Thank you for cooperating."

They'd gotten enough out of him for now. All they needed was to confirm the alibi. Taylor was suspicious of everything Chris was saying—he was still lying about stalking Olivia. But Taylor knew that if he had an alibi, then there was no way he could have killed Olivia. Their case against him was starting to crumble.

***

Outside in the briefing room, Taylor called Chris's mother, while Wesley took the job of checking with the other family members.

"So," Taylor said, her voice hasty. "Is it true that Chris was with you last night?"

"Yes, he was!" Mrs. Davy said, excited. "Why? Did—did something happen to him?"

"Did he tell you about Olivia?" Taylor asked.

"Is that the girl he had a crush on?"

Taylor almost laughed. Crush would be putting it lightly. But the fact that Chris's mom knew about Olivia told Taylor that his "crush" wasn't necessarily a secret.

"Right," Taylor said. "Olivia Newman was found dead this morning, and your son, Chris, has a history of stalking her."

"Stalking?" Mrs. Davy said, her voice raising in pitch. "Chris would never do that. Not my boy. Oh, my God, that poor girl…" Mrs. Davy choked on a sob. "What happened to her?"

Taylor didn't answer, because she was the one who needed answers. "Where was he last night?" Taylor asked.

"He was here all night," Mrs. Davy said. "We had a family gathering, and there are over a dozen people who can confirm Chris was here. My boy isn't a killer."

"He slept over?" Taylor pressed. "He didn't leave at all?"

"No," Mrs. Davy said. "We would have noticed if he left."

Damn. The alibi was checking out. They would have to confirm it with the other guests, and Taylor knew what lengths mothers would go to in order to protect their child. She could be lying. But Taylor's gut was telling her that Chris wasn't their guy.

"Thank you for your time," she said. "We'll be in touch." Then she hung up.

Across the briefing room, Wesley hung up his phone call too.

"Anything?" Taylor asked.

He shook his head. "Multiple witnesses state he was with them all night."

"His mother confirmed it too."

"So he's not our guy."

They both sighed. As creepy as Chris Davy was—that didn't make him a killer. Taylor was hoping for more progress than this.

Taylor and Wesley went back and stood outside of the interrogation room, both less convinced that Chris Davy was the one who had murdered Olivia Newman. They watched through the double-sided glass as Chris sulked in the interrogation room.

"Guess we have to believe him," Taylor told Wesley.

"Alibi checks out, whether I like it or not," Wesley said. "But the guy is still a scumbag creep."

"Agreed," Taylor said.

But what could they do next? Their case was falling apart, and their only suspect was starting to seem a little less like a suspect. They could ding him for stalking, but not for murder. That was more the type of work beat cops did than federal agents, and Taylor knew Winchester expected more from her—and her new partner.

Taylor sighed. She hated this feeling. She felt so close to finding out who killed Olivia, and now she was starting to make mistakes. She didn't want to rush things and get the wrong guy. But if Chris Davy wasn't the one, then who was?

"I think we need a break," Wesley said.

As much as Taylor hated to admit it, she was starting to agree. They were going in circles and were getting nowhere. Taylor had no other suspects to pursue, so they were at a stalemate.

But if they were breaking, then this was a good time for Taylor to bring up what happened earlier. She wasn't impressed with Wesley's stubbornness—not only with Chris, but with *her.*

Wesley was grabbing his jacket off the desk and slinging it over his shoulder when Taylor stopped him.

"Wesley."

He looked at her, gray eyes like metal. "What?"

Taylor almost wavered. Almost. She barely knew him, and she didn't like the way he intimidated her. But she wouldn't *show* she felt that way. She was an agent too, and as far as she was concerned, they were equals. Even if he did have height, age, and experience on her.

"We need to talk about what happened earlier."

"What happened?" Wesley lifted a bushy eyebrow.

"I was trying to go over a gameplan with you and you weren't open to my suggestions. Plus, was keeping your shoes on really that important? We should've tried harder to keep Chris calm."

"What for? We needed him to come down one way or another, and

31

I figured it'd be easier if we had a reason to cuff him."

Taylor couldn't believe what she was hearing. "So you provoked him on purpose?"

Wesley shrugged. "It worked, didn't it?"

Taylor didn't know what to say. Yes, it worked, although provoking somebody on purpose could be dangerous. Wesley hadn't been too aggressive with Chris. He'd just gently triggered him enough to make him throw the first punch. But still—Taylor should have known that going in.

"If that was the plan, I would have liked to know," Taylor said pointedly. "Intentionally provoking a perp could be dangerous for both of us."

"You're right, Sage, but when I saw him, I figured I could push a couple of his buttons, and it worked. It's not something I'd do recklessly with just anyone."

"Okay, but it's still something we should discuss *together.*"

Taylor could hardly believe *she* was giving somebody the teamwork talk. She'd always been the lone wolf type. But at least she tried to communicate with her partners instead of totally stonewalling them.

Maybe this thing with Wesley wasn't going to work, but Taylor couldn't risk looking unprofessional and complaining about her partner.

But then, to her surprise, Wesley softened up. His posture loosened, and he let out a sigh. "Special Agent Sage, listen," he began, running a hand along the back of his neck. "I apologize. I'm not used to working with others. I figured Chief Winchester would've warned you about that."

She eased off. His tone felt genuine, and Taylor was always willing to listen to someone if they were apologizing. "He didn't even give me your name," Taylor said. "You're still a mystery to me."

"You are too," Wesley said. "Sorry if we got off on the wrong foot, I'm just hyper-focused. That crime scene made me sick. Finding out who did it is all I'm concerned about right now."

Taylor understood that completely. In fact, Wesley's words sounded so familiar, she swore they could have been her own. Maybe they had more in common than she'd realized.

Feeling more confident, and like she understood him better, she nodded. This partnership needed work—but if Wesley was willing to work out the kinks with her, Taylor was willing to try.

Suddenly, there was a knock at the door. Chief Steven Winchester briskly walked into the room, a look of urgency on his face.

Taylor's stomach dropped. She knew what that meant.

"You two—no time for chit-chat," he said. "That dirtbag in there—he's not the killer."

Oh, no. If Winchester was saying that, it could only mean one thing.

He confirmed it by saying: "We found another body."

CHAPTER SEVEN

Taylor stood before her next crime scene with her stomach in knots. In the middle of a public park, under the shade of a tree, was a young woman lying as stiff as a mannequin.

And she was holding a ghost orchid.

Taylor and Wesley had just arrived. The cops surrounding the scene all wore grim faces, and some of them were familiar. They had been at the other crime scene earlier. In a small town like this, Taylor doubted most of these cops had ever seen the work of a serial killer, let alone twice within twenty-four-hours.

"When was she found?" Taylor asked one of the officers.

"An hour ago," the cop, a young guy, said grimly.

"And no one touched her?" Wesley asked him.

"No, sir."

Taylor looked back down at the victim. With her long brown hair and slender body, topped with a crop top, she encapsulated the beauty standards most young people seemed to idolize these days. She looked like somebody who Taylor would see with a million followers on social media.

"Do we have an ID?" Taylor asked.

"Zoe Duntz," the officer replied. "She... is a bit of a celebrity here."

Taylor's heart stopped.

A celebrity.

The last victim had been an actress. Small time, but still. This could be the connection.

"How so?" Taylor asked. "What did she do?"

"Social media, I think," the officer said. "I'm sorry, I don't know that much yet."

Taylor nodded. "Thank you," she said. They could do their recon later—for now, she needed to see more.

Taylor and Wesley stepped up to the scene. The girl was clearly beautiful. But now, her face was contorted in a grimace of terror. Her eyes, wide and staring, bulged out of her head. She had a pale, almost translucent complexion, like she was carved from marble. Although judging by the red flush still on her skin, this crime was fresh—maybe an hour or two old.

34

It was just as bad as Taylor had feared.

She knew Wesley felt the same. He kneeled outside the caution tape, looked down at the woman, and then stood up straight, swallowing hard. "It's the same," he said.

Taylor's mind reeled. There was no way this could be a coincidence. It was too similar, too well-planned.

It was official. They were chasing after a serial killer.

Taylor crouched down, reaching into her pocket for a pair of latex gloves. She snapped them on and stood up, walking over to the body. It was almost like she was getting ready to behead a snake. She hovered her hand over the victim's neck.

The shape of her strangulation mark was the same as the last one. The ribbon.

She looked around, trying to get a feel for the scene. It wasn't a very popular park. No one saw anything. But there was still a crowd on the other side of the caution tape, with their eyes fixed on the crime scene, all trying to catch a glimpse of what was going on, even though they weren't allowed.

As Taylor looked up, she noticed two boys standing by the fence, watching the scene.

That officer had mentioned Zoe was a social media celebrity, well known. She would have had many fans. Likely of the young male variety.

Taylor's mind went back to those two boys. They were hiding behind the fence, keeping their heads down, trying not to be noticed. They were too far to see what they looked like, but they were older than teenagers. The girl was in her twenties.

She walked over to the two boys and blocked their view of the crime scene. "What are your names?"

The boys looked up at her. It was clear they hadn't expected to be approached by an FBI agent. "B-Bryan," said one of them. He was tall, skinny, and had a mess of brown hair on his head. He looked awestruck, like he didn't know what to do with himself.

"You know this is a crime scene," Taylor said. "Is there a reason you're watching?"

"It's just..." The one boy trembled. "Isn't that Zoe Duntz?"

Taylor's mind reeled. She could feel the boys' eyes on her, as if they expected her to say something. To confirm what his friend had just said.

But Taylor wasn't about to make a public statement. If she did, it would be all over the news, and these boys, who might—*might*—have some information, would be gone. She wasn't about to let that happen.

"I can't tell you that," Taylor said.

But the boy said, "She had like ten million followers. Her top post was about how this park was the best in town 'cause it's so quiet," the other boy said. He was shorter and much skinnier, but still seemed strong. Based on the way his eyes were darting around, she could tell he was the nervous type.

Taylor glanced at the scene. The middle of the park was pretty, but there was nothing all that special about it. Quietness. Was that what someone like Zoe, with ten million followers, really wanted? Maybe it was the most secluded spot to take photos of herself without an audience.

Taylor looked back at the boys. "Well, I'm not sure, but thank you for the information," she said. "You aren't allowed to be here. Please leave."

The boys looked at each other, as if unsure what to do. But then they started walking, away from the scene and down the quiet street. Taylor watched them go and thought about the information they had given her.

Ten million followers wasn't nothing. In fact, that was incredible for a girl in such a small town. The fact that she had posted about the park before, too—that was good to know. What it told Taylor was that whoever did this was looking at Zoe's profile. Following her life. What it meant was that this was not a crime of passion or opportunity—it was as she'd suspected. A deliberate stalking.

Zoe wasn't random. Like Olivia, she had been selected.

Taylor walked back over to Wesley, who was talking to a couple officers. He broke away from them when he saw Taylor walking up, and they reconvened away from the ears of the officers.

"What was that about?" Wesley asked.

"Just some kids," Taylor said. "They recognized the victim. Turns out she was more than just a local celebrity. Her social media presence was in the millions."

"Millions of potential stalkers," Wesley said.

"Exactly. Did you find anything out?"

"Only that her family isn't in town—they're flying in from out of state, so we can't talk to them yet."

Taylor nodded. That was just her luck. But they could still learn a lot about Zoe from her social media profiles.

With a long sigh, she stared back at the crime scene, at the flower delicately placed in Zoe's hands. Why choose the ghost orchid? Did it symbolize that the victims themselves were "rare" in some way? Taylor wasn't sure. There could be more to the flower, more lore she wasn't aware of.

"I think we should chase down the flower lead while we wait for her parents to show up," Taylor told Wesley. "I'm struggling to figure out what it means."

"Agreed," Wesley said. "Any ideas where to start?"

Actually, Taylor did have one. Pine Point was only a thirty-minute drive from D.C.—and she knew there was someone there who happened to be an expert on this subject.

CHAPTER EIGHT

Taylor entered Bartholomae Park in Washington, D.C., amazed by the giant fountain that looked more like an extravagant chandelier spouting water. It was after two p.m. now, and starfruit-colored clouds painted the sky, basking the beautiful, lush park in a golden afternoon glow.

But Taylor wasn't here to admire the scenery. She was here to solve a murder.

Wesley walked behind her. Taylor had wanted to carpool, but the man had insisted on driving himself. They still hadn't fully warmed up to each other, but Taylor didn't care. As long as they got results, that was all that mattered. FBI agents didn't need to be best friends; they just needed to get the job done, put the criminal behind bars.

Taylor had set the meeting point with Jamie Delaine, a botany professor who had been a consultant for the FBI for a number of years. Taylor had heard of her before but had never had a need to meet with her. She'd never worked a case that involved flowers in this sense. But the ghost orchid left at each crime scene had to mean something. Taylor knew about their rarity, but she hoped Jamie would be able to shed some light.

Taylor and Wesley found Jamie on a park bench, wearing a white romper with overalls over it. The petite woman was in her forties, had long, blonde hair and green eyes that pierced through everything like a laser. Her hair was pulled up into a sleek, structured bun. She looked like she was ready to go to a gardening party. A pair of sparkling diamond studs twinkled in her ears, and her large, dark sunglasses shielded her face.

"Special Agent Sage, Special Agent Wesley," Jamie said with a small smile. She was holding a red notepad and pen. "Nice to meet you both."

Taylor tried to shake her hand, but Jamie didn't accept.

"Forgive me for not shaking hands," Jamie said, winking. "I've been gardening all day and I'm afraid my hands are filthy."

"It is no trouble at all," Taylor said.

"You've assisted the FBI before," Wesley noted.

"Oh yes," Jamie said. "I've helped many times. I know a thing or two about plants. I've been studying botany for nearly thirty years. I'm lucky enough to teach here while also working part-time at the most beautiful botany park in the world." Taylor knew Jamie was referring to the exact place they were standing, and Taylor couldn't deny the truth in her words—this was the most gorgeous park she'd ever seen too.

"I have a degree in psychology as well," Jamie said. "But I am far more interested in plants than people. I find them much more interesting. They're so honest and pure."

"Oh?" Taylor said, sitting next to her. She was fascinated to know more about what had led Jamie to be a professor, a gardener, and an FBI consultant.

"Yes," Jamie said. "They don't have ulterior motives. They don't have secondary goals. They're just happy to be themselves. I enjoy the study of plants more than the study of people, to be honest. It's so much easier to understand them. They're very black and white. If you give them the right care, they will thrive. They will bloom and bring beauty into the world. It's a wonderful process to be a part of."

Taylor couldn't help but admire Jamie. If only her own life were simple enough in knowing so much about people but choosing to focus on flowers instead.

But with all respect to Jamie, Taylor wasn't here to talk about her.

"We were hoping you could shed some light on the ghost orchid," Taylor said. "We've found two of them at two different crime scenes."

"Oh, that's interesting. The ghost orchid is very rare. I know of only a few places in the world that grow it. They're very mysterious flowers. They tend to bloom in June and July and are endemic to South Florida and Cuba."

"Why June and July?" Taylor wondered. "Because it's even hotter?"

"But there are more factors to it than just temperature," Jamie said. "If a plant doesn't have the right conditions for growth, it won't bloom. The flower will remain in the bud stage for its entire life. For example, many orchids grow in a certain type of tree bark. They will stay in that tree trunk until they die. So some of the variables that the ghost orchid needs are unknown. It's no wonder they are so rare."

"Interesting," Taylor said.

"They tend to grow very well in Hawaii because they're growing in similar conditions to their original place of growth," Jamie continued. "They prefer warm weather and very humid, wet conditions. They have no leaves, so they require a lot of water."

"Could one be grown here?"

"In the right conditions, sure," Jamie said. "But not easily, and certainly not outdoors."

A pause hung in the air. Taylor listened to the sound of bees buzzing around in the garden surrounding them. Wesley had taken the backseat on the conversation, as he seemed to have even less of an interest in flowers than Taylor did.

"It's a beautiful flower," Taylor murmured. "But as I mentioned, we've found one on two bodies so far."

"That is unusual," Jamie said. "What's more, the ghost orchid is not the kind of flower that you would associate with... murder. She's not a dark flower. She's a harmless, delicate flower. A symbol of peace and serenity. It's disturbing that such a beauty would be used in this way. It seems highly unlikely that anyone would have such easy access to this flower, so I do wonder how they were able to access it."

Taylor nodded. As suspected, the ghost orchid was not readily available or easy to grow.

Which meant that whoever was doing this had to have some sort of expertise in botany, assuming they were growing the flower themselves, which seemed possible, considering how difficult it was to access otherwise. It wasn't something you could simply go to the store and buy.

Maybe they would be better off looking into specialists in the field. People who knew their stuff, who might have easier access to the flower.

"I was just wondering if you've heard of any botanists or other specialists who might be able to grow this flower," Taylor said.

"That's a hard one," Jamie said. "There are many in D.C. who might have the experience to grow such a rare and mysterious flower. It's possible. But I do think that if someone is that knowledgeable about the flower, they probably already have one. Or two."

Jamie and Taylor shared a look. Taylor knew exactly what the other woman was thinking; that the killer could very well be growing the flower themselves.

"I would try the Botanical Garden here in D.C.," Jamie said. "I've heard they have them there, although I spend most days here."

Taylor nodded. That sounded like a plan. "Thank you, Jamie."

Suddenly, Taylor's phone buzzed in her pocket. "Excuse me," she said and stepped away, leaving Wesley with Jamie. Winchester was calling.

"Chief, what's going on?" Taylor asked into the phone.

"You two should get back to HQ," Winchester said. "The victim's parents are here."

They were already in D.C., and Taylor had wanted to run down that lead—but talking to Zoe's parents was important, too.

"We'll be there, Chief," Taylor said. The second Taylor hung up, she called Wesley over. "We need to head back to HQ," Taylor said.

Taylor tried to keep the excitement from her face, but she had that gut feeling again: the one that told her they were onto something good. This was a breakthrough. They were close. They could solve this thing.

They were going to catch the Ghost Orchid Killer.

CHAPTER NINE

Taylor stormed into Quantico with Wesley, eager to talk to Zoe Duntz's parents—and find out if there was more to the connection between her and the first victim. To see if they could help her get closer to the killer. They found Zoe's parents in the briefing room, seated at the table. Winchester stood when she and Wesley entered.

"Sage, Wesley—glad you're here," Winchester said. "Ms. Duntz's parents flew in all the way from Arkansas."

Taylor's eyes fell on Zoe's parents. They were clearly destroyed over the death of their daughter—tears stained their cheeks, and their heads were held low. Winchester looked relieved that he could get out of there and leave the dirty work of talking to the parents to Taylor and Wesley. He left the room quietly. Taylor and Wesley sat down opposite them.

"Mr. and Mrs. Duntz," Taylor said. "I'm Special Agent Sage. I'm here to help find your daughter's killer."

"I still can't believe my little girl is dead," Mrs. Duntz said. "Who would do this?"

"I know," Taylor said. "We're going to do everything we can to bring her killer to justice."

"My daughter was so influen—" Mr. Duntz cut himself off. "She was loved by all of her followers. People even paid to follow her. She was loved by thousands of people."

"I'm sure your daughter had an impact on everyone she came into contact with," Taylor said. "If you could be more specific, the more I know about Zoe, the more we can focus our investigation on people who might have wanted to hurt her."

"This is so terrible," Mrs. Duntz said. "Our Zoe would never do anything to hurt anyone. She was--just beautiful."

"We know," Wesley cut in abruptly. "And it's our job to make sure justice is served for her."

"We know you don't want to hear this," Taylor added on, "but there may be more to this than meets the eye. So we'd like to know more about who Zoe was." Taylor pulled out a notebook. "What was she like?"

"She was beautiful and kind," Mrs. Duntz said. "She was a dancer, for a while. I took her to her first ballet class when she was just a little baby. She loved to dance. She was very good, too. She wanted to be a ballerina when she grew up. She said she wanted to wear a tutu and be on stage. We were so proud of her."

"She wanted to be a ballerina?" Taylor asked. Nothing on Zoe's social media had hinted at that. In fact, Zoe seemed to be more into the beach and partying than anything else. Not that a person's social media could ever encapsulate their whole life.

"Yes, when she was a child," Zoe's father said, placing a hand on his wife's shoulder. "But she lost interest when she got older."

"She had such talent," Mrs. Duntz said. "But as she grew up, she changed her mind. All she cared about was her social media."

"Her damn social media, which we always knew could attract the wrong kind of attention," Mr. Duntz said. "She got angry messages sometimes too."

Taylor's ears perked. "Angry how?"

"People accused Zoe of altering her photos," Mrs. Duntz said.

"Altering her photos? What do you mean?" Taylor asked. This detail could be significant.

"Zoe had Photoshop," Mr. Duntz said. "She would alter her photos before she put them up online. It's all about how many followers you can get these days. If you have more followers, everyone wants to be you. Everyone wants to be around you."

"Zoe was very popular," Mrs. Duntz said. "We didn't even know how many followers she had. The internet is—it's a different world."

"She had an upwards of ten million," Taylor told them.

Their eyes widened.

"I didn't know it had gotten that out of hand," Mr. Duntz said. "Zoe received a lot of nasty messages from people. I told her to stop using Photoshop, but she wanted to be popular, and she felt like that was the only way."

Something about that struck a familiar chord. She wanted to be popular, and felt like that was the only way...

Just like Olivia Newman and her nose job.

"She was a sweet girl," Mrs. Duntz said. "But she had a lot of issues."

"Issues?" Wesley asked.

"With her weight," Mr. Duntz said. "Zoe always felt like she was too fat. Even though she wasn't. She thought she was too fat, so she starved herself."

"We tried dieting for her," Mrs. Duntz said. "But—"

43

"Zoe just wanted to be perfect," Mr. Duntz said. "Perfect skin, perfect frame. She wanted everyone to love her."

"It wasn't just about the looks," Mrs. Duntz said. "Zoe always felt like she didn't fit in. She wanted everyone to accept her. She didn't have her own identity. Everything was about being popular. It—it even made her anxious sometimes."

"Anxious?" Taylor asked.

"It's funny," Mrs. Duntz said. "She was a very anxious child, but she was always calm about her popularity. She didn't like her anxiety. She felt like she was broken. She said she wasn't normal. She felt like she was the only person in the world that had these problems."

"Sounds like she was suffering from generalized anxiety," Taylor said. In that sense, she felt for Zoe. It didn't matter how happy someone looked online—there was always something darker going on beneath the surface. It wasn't uncommon for people to fabricate identities on social media. In fact, Taylor blamed it for a lot of the depression that plagued today's young people.

Taylor thought of herself, for a moment; she didn't have social media, but she did put on a brave face at work, always hiding what was going on at home. She hadn't even told Winchester, or anyone, that Ben had left her. Figured it wasn't their business or would make them think she was less capable of doing her job. And Taylor couldn't have that.

"You're right. That's what Zoe said too," Mrs. Duntz said.

Taylor nodded. "And you can't think of anyone specific who Zoe had issues with? Any one stalker?"

"Not that we know of," Mr. Duntz said.

Having learned enough, Taylor said, "Thank you for your time. And we're sorry again for your loss."

"Thank you," Mrs. Duntz said, before she burst into tears and threw her arms around her husband. Taylor left the parents alone to grieve in the briefing room.

Once alone in the hallway, Taylor faced Wesley. She sighed and put her hands on her hips.

"I don't know if Zoe's anxiety or social media presence contributed to her death," Taylor said. "Olivia Newman didn't have a massive following, or a following who was angry with her."

"Not that we know of," Wesley said.

"There was one thing that stood out, though." Taylor paused, running over their options in her mind. "Olivia Newman had plastic surgery. Zoe Duntz altered her pictures."

"There could be a connection there," Wesley said.

"Exactly… but I'm not sure what we can do with it yet."

While the conversation with the parents had shed a stronger light on who Zoe was as a person, Taylor couldn't think of any way it pointed at her killer.

No. For now, the lead they'd uncovered with Jamie seemed to be the strongest.

Their next destination could only be the Botanical Gardens.

CHAPTER TEN

Taylor entered the Botanical Gardens greenhouse with Wesley, running over the killer's profile in her mind. There had to be a connection between the two victims, and Taylor began to form an image of what it might be. Photoshopping and plastic surgery—they were both about altering one's natural appearance. Taylor still didn't know exactly what that said about the killer, but she intended to find out.

The smell of greenery filled her nostrils. Wesley was quiet beside her as they paced past the greenery. As before, he had insisted that they each drive their own cars; Taylor wasn't sure why he was so against carpooling, but she remembered what he'd said earlier—that he wasn't used to working with others. This was only their first day working together, and Taylor figured they both needed time to warm up.

Taylor approached an employee, who was reading off some sort of clipboard—likely a tour guide waiting to show people around.

"Excuse me," Taylor began politely. The girl looked up at both Taylor and Wesley in shock. "We're with the FBI. We called ahead about talking to the head of the ghost orchid exhibit."

"Oh, yes, you're looking for Murray. Let me take you to him."

They followed the girl around several aisles of plants. Despite the warmth of the greenhouse, the humidity made Taylor's hair frizz up instantly. The young woman led them to a door leading to another greenhouse. She knocked and opened it. A heavyset man with graying hair looked up from a flower he was observing.

"This is Dr. Brandon Murray," the employee said before she left.

"Hello. Thanks for agreeing to meet with us so quickly," Taylor said, shaking his hand.

Murray motioned for the agents to follow him through the greenhouse. "You said you were investigating the murder of a young woman. Are you close to finding the killer?"

"If we were, we wouldn't be here," Wesley said.

Taylor shot him a look that he promptly ignored. Clearing her throat, she told Murray, "Unfortunately, the only real lead we have right now is the ghost orchid the killer has been leaving on each victim. You're the one in charge of taking care of the ones you have here,

46

right?"

"Oh, yes, it's a finicky little flower," the man said. "I have no idea how the guy you're after could get his hands on one. Let alone two."

"Maybe he's a regular here?" Wesley asked.

"We have thousands of visitors to the gardens every day, but the flowers are kept in quarantine," Murray replied. "You'd have better luck stealing the Mona Lisa."

"Do you mind if we take a look at one?" Taylor asked.

"Of course. This way," Murray led them to a glass case with a group of ghost orchids inside. Behind the misted glass, the white, curvy flowers sent a chill up Taylor's spine. What was supposed to be beautiful now made her think of death.

"Only the ones we have are kept here," Murray said. "These are the ones visitors can see."

Taylor nodded. "And you said there's no chance any could be stolen?"

"Not at all. I keep track of them myself."

"Are you sure you can keep them all safe?" Wesley's voice grew hard.

Murray bristled. "Look, those flowers are my life. I promise you two, none were taken. So whoever had those flowers didn't get them from here. It does surprise, me, though—these things are extremely hard to grow. So whoever has them... he must know his stuff. Otherwise, the flowers would just die."

Taylor and Wesley exchanged a look before Taylor asked, "Who has access to this area besides yourself?"

Murray frowned. "The conservatory workers. Some of the gardeners. And some of the members of my team. But I don't think any of them would be able to steal one."

"You have a team of people taking care of these flowers?" Wesley asked.

"Yes. It's not just me. I have a horticulturist, an entomologist, a botanist, and two apprentices."

Taylor glanced at Wesley. "So, six people total? Anyone else?"

"No. That's it. You can talk to the rest of my team, but I can guarantee you that none of them took those flowers."

"What do you think?" Taylor asked Wesley.

"It's worth looking into," Wesley admitted. He faced Murray again. "What about your employees?"

Murray shrugged. "They're all good people. But I don't see how one of them could have stolen one of the flowers. Like I said, the flower wasn't stolen from here... so, in my honest opinion, you should probably be looking for someone with knowledge on growing them himself."

Taylor stewed on it for a moment. Murray was probably right; she could go around with Wesley and interrogate every single employee in the building, but that would be time-consuming, and not all would be botany experts—the person who'd led them here was a simple tour guide.

No. It was probably best to get the techs back at HQ to come up with a list of employees here, and then go through each of them to determine if they had the expertise that would warrant an interview. On top of that, Taylor could hit two birds with one stone and get them to come up with a list of people with botany degrees in the area of Pine Point.

As Taylor and Wesley thanked Murray for his time, they exited the greenhouse and made their way through the indoor garden until they were back outside, where more lush greenery surrounded them, as well as visitors walking around and taking photos.

Taylor needed to go over her plan with Wesley. As they were walking back to the parking lot, she said, "Hey, Wesley, I think we need to let the techs do some recon for us, compile a list of names to interview. Employees who work here with significant knowledge, as well as anyone in the Pine Point area who might have a degree in botany or a related field."

Wesley looked at her. "You really think the killer is a botanist?"

"I don't know. But I'd like to know which ones exist in the area. And if they do, I want to talk to them. You never know what a person's thoughts could lead to. Evidence we might have missed. We have to consider every possibility."

"Fine. I'll let the techs know."

"Thanks."

When they reached their cars, Wesley paused. His eyes met hers, and he opened his mouth to speak, but then shut it. "Well, I guess I'll see you back at the headquarters," he said. "First thing tomorrow morning, okay?"

"Wait, tomorrow? Why not tonight?"

Wesley crossed his arms. "It's getting late, Sage. It's gonna take the techs hours to come up with that list. I have to get home. Don't you?"

Taylor thought about what was waiting for her at home. A huge, empty house with no husband. A cold bed. A barely stocked fridge. Ben always did all the cooking, and lately she'd been living off ramen noodles and spaghetti like she was a college student again.

But Wesley was right; it was going to take hours to get those names. Maybe a fresh start first thing in the morning would be good.

"Great work today," Taylor told him. "It was good to work with you."

Wesley looked away but nodded. "You too."

With that, he got into his car. Taylor sighed and got into hers too, buckling the seatbelt.

She sat alone with her thoughts for a moment. Lately, when she felt lost like this, there was only one place she wanted to go. It was like an addiction, going to the tarot reader's shop. But Taylor hadn't been able to totally shake her from her head all day.

Taylor groaned in frustration. She put the car in drive and sped out of the parking lot. She knew where she needed to be, but more importantly, she knew what she needed to do.

***

The bell to Miriam Belasco's shop dinged above Taylor's head as she entered. Belasco appeared through the curtain, looking tired—it was almost closing time, after all. Taylor had gone over the speed limit to make it here in time, and Belasco probably hadn't expected to see her again. Maybe she hoped she wouldn't.

"Mrs. Sage," Belasco said. "Did I not suggest taking a break from readings?"

"I'm sorry," Taylor said. She didn't know what else to say. Part of her was still embarrassed that she regularly visited a tarot reader. But Belasco had helped on more than one case now. And maybe, if Belasco couldn't give her any information on her husband or her missing sister, then she could at least give her some information on the case. Taylor was trying to catch a serial killer; that was her top priority.

"I'm not here on personal matters," Taylor said. "This is work-related."

Belasco's eyes slowly took her in. "And you're hoping for another reading?"

Taylor nodded. "You've helped me before. Maybe I never told you that, but... you did."

"I know." A smile tugged at Belasco's lips. "It's not that I'm not happy to help you, Mrs. Sage, but I worry about you. I worry my readings have given you hope about things I can't accurately predict. I can... see things sometimes, but the images aren't always literal."

49

Taylor knew she was referring to Angie. It was true—the readings had given her hope. But as much as Taylor wanted to ask Belasco to look deeper, try to find more, that wasn't why she came here.

"It's just work," Taylor said. "I promise."

"Very well, then. Follow me."

Taylor followed Belasco through the curtain, to the table at the back, where the tarot cards were set up. They assumed their positions: Taylor on one side, Belasco on the other. Belasco began shuffling the cards, then sorted them into three piles.

"Tell me," Belasco said, "do you have a specific question for the cards?"

Taylor thought on it for a moment. "I never knew how to ask you how you're getting this information," Taylor said as the silence stretched on. "But I've been finding out all kinds of things that I have no idea how you'd know."

Belasco sighed. "You're an FBI agent. I'm a fortune teller. I don't need to explain myself."

"I know that." Taylor paused. "I'll be direct. I'm hoping you can help give me a clue about the case I'm working."

"You mean you're hoping the cards can," Belasco said.

Taylor swallowed nervously. "Sure."

"Okay," Belasco breathed out. "Let's begin, then."

She flipped up the first card. "The Tower." Her voice was soft and steady. "This is sudden, unexpected change. Your unexpected change is coming. It's more than you expect, and it's more than you want."

"That's vague," Taylor said. Then again, Belasco's readings always were.

Belasco flipped the second card. "The Four of Swords. Upright. Stay calm, stay still, and think. There's no rush. You have all the time in the world to think."

Taylor took in Belasco's words. She truly always was in a rush. Rushing to solve the case. Rushing to fix things that could never be fixed. It seemed there was never enough time in the day for her.

But what did any of this have to do with the case?

Belasco flipped the third card. "The Moon," Belasco said. "You're not seeing the whole picture. Your mind is clouded, either by yourself or by an outside force, and you're not seeing the whole picture. The Moon also represents confusion and deception. There are lies."

"Who is lying?" Taylor asked, her heart pounding in her chest. Could it be Ben? Wesley?

One of the people she'd interviewed?

"I can't say for sure," Belasco said. A heavy pause hung in the air. "I will be honest, Mrs. Sage. This morning took a lot out of me, and I'm quite tired. I'm afraid I'm not fully open to the cards right now."

In all the time Taylor had known Belasco, she had never seemed so worn out. It would be cruel and selfish to push her more.

"Understood," Taylor said. "Thanks for your time." She rose to her feet, trying not to let her disappointment show on her face. She'd come all the way here for nothing.

"Take care of yourself, Mrs. Sage. And remember what I said: there's no rush. There's all the time in the world."

Taylor stepped out of Belasco's shop, into the warm night air. It was nearly nine o'clock. She would be getting home late. But she had to keep trying. There was a case to solve. There was a killer to catch. She couldn't give up now. But until she had another lead to run down, she forced herself to go home and rest, so she'd be fully recharged.

Tomorrow would be another day.

***

That night, Taylor didn't dream at all. In a weird way, she'd been sleeping better since Ben left her; she didn't have to lie awake and worry about if he was mad at her as he slept in the guest room. She knew he was gone, and so she could quietly drift away, trying to suppress her own nightmares on her own terms.

They still came sometimes. Some nights, she dreamt of Angie. Others, of the people in her life she'd lost. Like Calvin.

But Taylor had always been a restless sleeper, and the next morning, she awoke fifteen minutes before her alarm was meant to go off at six a.m. As she tossed and turned, Belasco's words spiraled in her mind—somebody was lying to her.

But who?

Just as Taylor was about to leave her bed, her phone on her nightstand rang. It was Wesley.

"This is Taylor Sage," she answered.

"Sage, you sound awake," Wesley said.

"Always am, Wesley."

"Good." He paused. "How long will it take you to get to HQ? We have a new suspect. Some employee at the Botanical Garden Production Facility."

Taylor immediately shot out of bed, heart in her throat. "Give me an hour."

CHAPTER ELEVEN

Taylor stormed into the Botanical Garden Production Facility with Wesley on her tail. This time, on the drive up, Wesley had actually been open to sharing a car with Taylor—biding that he was behind the wheel. But that was fine; Taylor didn't mind letting others drive, as it gave her time to think about the case and go over the files. The whole drive up, she'd been studying the case file on a certain employee at the production facility: Terrance Maxwell.

Now, they were here to track him down. His file had been clean, barring one thing: he had been accused of stalking a woman once before, although it was never proven, and the charges were eventually dropped. He had been with the company for about a year, and at the time of his hiring, there were two applicants for the job. Both were interviewed, but only Maxwell was hired.

Today, he was a security guard here in the Botanical Garden Production Facility. As they entered the building, they stopped at the reception desk.

"We're here to see Terrance Maxwell," Taylor said, showing her badge.

"Oh, right this way, Agents," the receptionist said, leading them down a long hallway.

The sound of their footsteps echoed through the hallway; it was dimly lit, but there was still a hint of sunlight that managed to slip in through the cracks of the blinds. They turned a corner, and a few more short strides brought them to the security office.

"Can I help you?" the man at the desk asked as they entered.

"We're here to see Terrance Maxwell," Taylor replied.

The man got up and came around the desk, extending a hand. "Hi, I'm Gary, Terrance's boss. Terrance isn't in today."

"Where is he?" Taylor pressed. Considering Terrance was involved in the world of botany, and had been charged with stalking before, that put him at the top of her list. Taylor didn't have time to screw around—she needed to talk to him stat.

"It's his day off," Gary said.

Damn it, Taylor thought. She wanted to talk to Terrance now. But maybe this wasn't such a bad thing—they could ask around about him, see if his fellow employees could dish out any dirt that might allude to his guilt. Gathering information on a suspect was always useful, as much as Taylor would rather be interrogating him.

Taylor shot Wesley a look and a nod, hoping he'd understand what she meant. She hadn't worked with him for long enough to have non-verbal communication—but Wesley had also proven to be incredibly intuitive behind his steely exterior.

He seemed to understand, because he faced Gary and said, "What can you tell us about Terrance?"

"Is he in trouble?" Gary asked. "Can I ask what this is about?"

"We're just looking into him," Taylor replied. "We can't give details right now."

"Now if you could answer my question," Wesley said. His domineering aura caused Gary to gulp.

Gary looked back and forth between them. "Well... Terrance is a bit of a weird kid. He keeps to himself."

"So he doesn't have many friends?" Taylor asked.

"Not really," Gary said. "He's that kid that everyone talks about behind his back, but nobody actually knows. I'm the only one who talks to him, though. I'm the only one who shows him any kindness. He's... well, look, Terrance is kinda like me. I was picked on when I was growing up; others made fun of me. But Terrance... he's different. Do you see what I'm saying? He's insanely smart, but he doesn't care about that."

"What do you mean by 'he doesn't care about that?'" Taylor asked.

"He doesn't care about being smart," Gary explained. "He doesn't care about the things other people care about. He's not a materialist."

Interesting choice of words. But there was one thing at the forefront of Taylor's mind: "Did Terrance know much about botany, or was he just a security guard here by chance?"

"Oh, Terrance loves plants," Gary said. "I can't even keep a succulent alive, but Terrance—"

"What about a ghost orchid?" Wesley pressed. He stepped up, his size causing Gary to shrink away. Taylor wasn't sure if the physical intimidation was intentional or not—but it seemed to get people talking.

"I don't know anything about that," Gary said. "Did Terrance do something bad? The FBI wouldn't be looking into him for nothing, right?"

Wesley looked like he wanted to press more, but Taylor stepped in: "That's fine, Gary. Thank you."

"But we're going to need Terrance's home address," Wesley said.

"And his phone number. I want to question him directly. It's the fastest way to get the answers we need."

"I don't know how to feel about that," Gary said. "Is he in trouble?"

"We can't say for sure," Wesley replied. "But it's better to be safe than sorry, right?"

"I guess you're right," Gary said. "I'll give you Terrance's info. But he could be in danger, you know, with you guys looking into him. I hope he doesn't end up getting hurt."

"We're just doing our job," Wesley replied. "The FBI's job. And that's to protect citizens, too."

Gary scribbled down the information and handed it to them. "Please be careful, Agents."

"We will," Taylor replied.

***

Taylor's chest felt tight as Wesley pulled his car up at the edge of the property, out in the countryside between D.C. and Pine Point. It was the perfect middle ground; if Terrance was the killer, he could easily drive to Pine Point to murder, then be back in time to drive in to work.

Plus, there was so much land here that it looked more like an old farm. The house and barn were far from the road and there were large hills and trees all around. Taylor wondered if this was how a farm looked in the 1800s. The house was tiny, not much more than a cabin. Two stories high, with a porch that extended all the way around. The house looked like it had been there for at least a hundred and fifty years.

There were no vehicles in the drive, and nothing seemed out of place. But it was eerily quiet; even the animals were strangely silent. If Terrance was inside, he wasn't showing it.

"This place gives me the creeps," Taylor said.

"Do you want me to call for backup?" Wesley asked.

"No, let's just take a look around." Taylor got out of the car, easing into the morning sun. Wesley got out after her. If they could find any sign of ghost orchids growing on this property, or anything else overly suspicious, then they'd have a real reason to bring Terrance in for questioning.

They walked to the side of the house and found a small vegetable garden with a variety of herbs growing. No sign of any ghost orchids, but of course, Jamie had said it would be near impossible to grow them outdoors. The ghost orchid took great care, which meant if Terrance did have one, it was likely growing inside one of these buildings somewhere.

Taylor walked around to the side of the garage. Wesley followed after her.

There was a door to the side of the garage, like an over-sized door for a fridge or freezer. Taylor tried the handle, but it was locked. There was a second door, right next to it, also locked.

Little things about the property were starting to signal red flags to Taylor. For one, across the yard, there were a series of soda cans. Taylor was sure Terrance had been using them for target practice with a rifle. The point was that these were things that didn't really fit with the image of a caring botanist. Taylor wanted to solve this case—she wanted to be the one to bring down the killer.

All she could do was follow the evidence.

Admission to the house wouldn't be easy, but the barn was at the edge of the property, up against the forest. Taylor headed straight for the barn, but she could hear Wesley on her six. He was being overly cautious. But then she wasn't surprised; everything about Wesley told her he was a veteran agent.

"Terrance?" Taylor called. She turned and looked at Wesley. "You stay here. Keep an eye out."

"Yes, ma'am." His lips were pressed together, but there was a twinkle in his eye. Taylor appreciated that he was stepping back and letting her take the lead—it probably wasn't easy for him. She made a mental note to thank him later.

She opened the door of the barn, just a crack so that it wouldn't squeak on its ancient hinges. The air inside smelled musty and sweet, like roses and chrysanthemums. Well, that made sense. Terrance would have a greenhouse.

Her heart rate picked up. If the ghost orchid was anywhere—it had to be here.

But just as Taylor went to move her foot, to actually step inside, something clicked beneath her. She froze in place.

She recognized that sound, and it turned every muscle in her body to concrete.

"Sage," Wesley said, his voice ice cold. "Do not move."

Taylor's heart fell to the floor.

She looked down to see her foot was pressed firmly on top of a pressure plate.

CHAPTER TWELVE

She didn't move. Couldn't move. Her foot was so heavy on the plate, she could barely think.

"It's rigged with a bomb," Wesley said, his voice deadly calm. Taylor's stomach filled with panic. She wanted to throw up.

She'd been shot before, but somehow, this felt the closet to death she'd ever been. One wrong move of her foot and she was a goner.

"Sage," Wesley said. Taylor focused on his voice.

"I'm not going to fucking move, Wesley," Taylor said, trying to stay calm. She'd been trained to deal with situations such as this, but that didn't make it any less terrifying. "Call the bomb squad, now," she said. *Keep calm. Stay focused.*

"On it." Wesley already had the phone to his ear.

Taylor shut her eyes and tried to revert into her happy place as Wesley gave the bomb squad the directions. *Happy thoughts. Think happy thoughts...*

But it was easier said than done, and fear took over again. Taylor began sweating buckets. She needed to get her foot off this thing.

If Belasco was able to warn her about anything, she wished it had been this. How could Taylor have a future with a child if she was meant to die today? How could she ever find Angie?

"Sage." Wesley's voice returned. "Stay calm, okay? They're on their way. You're gonna be okay. Just listen to my voice."

"I've got it." Taylor took a breath. She was on the verge of tears, but no matter the situation, she didn't want to show weakness to her new partner. She didn't want him to know that her life, and her many potential futures, were flickering away in front of her eyes.

She thought of her childhood, back when Angie was still around. She found herself smiling. She couldn't stop. She pictured the two of them as little girls, making mud pies and squealing with delight when they were cleaned up.

One day, she was going to be a mother. She was going to hold her child in her lap and smile, just like she was smiling now. She was going to be a mother.

But if she moved her foot, none of that would ever happen.

Keep calm. Think happy thoughts. Not the best time to get

sentimental.

More memories flooded Taylor's mind. She remembered the time Angie was teaching her how to ride a bike, and she'd fallen over and skinned her knee. She'd felt so dumb. Not Angie, who was always the more athletic one. Taylor had been the more studious one. That's because Angie had her, the smart one, to help her with her homework and with her art. She'd always been Angie's rock. And Angie was her rock, too.

Taylor remembered in high school, when Taylor had her first crush on a boy—Angie had encouraged Taylor to ask him out. She did, and she was rejected.

Angie let that boy have it.

Taylor had been so embarrassed, but she wished more than anything that Angie were here right now to call Ben out for being such a terrible husband.

Every memory of Angie had always felt like a punch in the gut. Taylor had wanted to find her sister for so long that, even though it was years later, all of those feelings were still there.

If Taylor moved her foot, she'd never find her sister.

"Sorry, I forgot who I was talking to," Wesley said. "Of course you're tough as nails."

Taylor was pulled back to the present, acutely aware of the danger. "Wesley, I'd really rather not die here."

"You're not going to die," Wesley said, his voice calm and soothing. "You're just stuck beside a barn until the bomb squad comes."

"How comforting." Taylor let out a sigh. She tried to relax, tried to focus on her happy place, but the pressure plate was still under her foot, and it felt like a hot plate burning her. Her stomach churned with anxiety.

Why the hell hadn't she been more thorough? She'd been so focused on the idea of this being Terrance's land, she'd not really even considered the possibility of a booby trap. She breathed deeply and tried to calm her nerves. She was a trained FBI agent; she was supposed to be able to deal with situations such as this.

It didn't work.

Her chest tightened and breathing became difficult. She could feel the sweat running down her face and she could hear her heartbeat thrumming in her head.

She looked up at Wesley and saw the fear in his eyes.

"Sage, it's gonna be okay," Wesley said.

Taylor focused on Wesley. He was right. *I've got this. I know what*

I'm doing. But her heart was pounding in her chest and her breathing was coming in short gasps.

"Breathe. Inhale. Good girl. Now exhale. That's it."

Taylor focused on his voice, and she tried to do what he said. A few seconds later, her breathing returned to normal. She risked a glance out of the corner of her eye. Wesley was watching her, his eyes intent. She held out her hand and nodded.

"You need to back up and keep your distance."

"I'm not leaving you alone," Wesley said.

"Noble of you, but—"

"No buts," Wesley snapped, his eyes as hard as steel. "You're gonna be okay. And I'm not going anywhere."

Taylor smiled. He was brave. Braver than she'd given him credit for.

The minutes felt like an eternity. At long last, Taylor heard the sound of trucks arriving, the engines rumbling and tires crunching over stones.

The squad was here.

Taylor could breathe again. Within minutes, a group of men wearing flak jackets cautiously approached them. But the danger wasn't over yet—they still had to deal with this damn thing.

"Special Agent Sage, we're going to need you to stay calm," one man said.

"Oh, I'm very calm," Taylor insisted.

"We'll get you out of this. I promise. We're going to diffuse the bomb now, okay? We need you to keep the pressure on it until we say so."

"Got it," Taylor said. She kept her pressure on the plate, holding back a wince. It all felt surreal. Like any second, her entire life could flash away. Every ounce of trust she had went into these men as they did their work. Taylor shut her eyes and listened but couldn't look; it was like being operated on with no anesthesia.

Finally, one man said, "Okay, Special Agent Sage, you can lift your foot now."

"Are you sure?" Taylor's breathing was labored.

"Positive. You're safe."

Carefully, Taylor lifted her foot.

And nothing happened.

She let out a breath. It was a relief to feel it finally move. Thank God—she was safe.

"Okay, Agent Sage, take a step back now."

Taylor stepped away and watched as the bomb squad began working on the device. They pulled it out and looked at the wiring, taking pictures and measurements. It was a very delicate process, and a large part of Taylor wanted to follow after them and be nosy. But she stayed in place and turned to face Wesley. The whole thing felt like a bad dream: the pressure plate, the thoughts that had run through Taylor's head.

"You did good, Sage," Wesley said.

Taylor nodded, although she was still shaken up. "Thanks, Wesley. I couldn't have done it alone."

"Balls," Wesley said. "You had this under control, Sage. You did good."

Taylor smiled at him, relieved she had made it out okay, and that Wesley was proving to be a reliable partner. He had handled this well—calm, level-headed, and with kindness at that. Taylor had felt as safe as she possibly could with a bomb under her foot as Wesley had talked her down.

That took trust. Trust that Taylor realized was quickly building with him.

But the work wasn't over yet.

Whatever was in that barn was clearly worth protecting. Taylor had every intention of continuing her search—this wasn't enough to break her resolve. Not even close.

Taylor asked the bomb squad to do a quick sweep of the area, and they determined no more booby traps were set up, but to be careful anyway, just in case. They stood by as Taylor and Wesley finally entered the barn, which was actually a disguised greenhouse.

The plants were gorgeous. They were all perfectly tended, perfectly organized. The scent of roses was nice, but there was something else in the air, something that made Taylor's nostrils flare.

"Smells like pot," Wesley noted. "We'll need to—"

"Damn," Taylor swore, placing a hand over her nose. She'd always been sensitive to the smell of weed—and she could make out the tall shapes of pot plants across the barn.

"What?" Wesley asked.

"Over there. That looks like a lot of marijuana."

"It sure looks like it," Wesley said.

"Damn, Terrance."

"He's going down for it, Sage. No doubt about that." Wesley shook his head. "So what should we bag him for? Possession? Trafficking?"

"With his criminal history—and now this—I think we could bag him for something much bigger." Taylor faced Wesley. "Let's ping his cellphone and hunt him down."

***

Taylor eyed the man in front of her. Terrance Maxwell sat across from her in the interrogation room at Quantico HQ, his face shielded by his long bangs. They'd pinged his cellphone and found him at a diner, immediately taking him down to HQ, despite his protests. All in all, though, Terrance was a sulky young man in all black, and not much of a talker.

Wesley was beside Taylor, and he'd been spearheading the interrogation. So far, they'd gotten nothing out of him. And Taylor could tell Wesley was losing his patience.

"Cut the shit," Wesley said. "You nearly got charged for stalking a woman before, Terrance. You almost killed my partner here with your little trap."

"Look," Terrance said, sounding tired, "I already told you, I was growing the weed medicinally. I don't know anything else. I didn't stalk anybody."

Taylor gauged Terrance's reaction. He admitted to the weed, but they hadn't told him the real reason he was in yet: on suspicion of the murders of Olivia Newman and Zoe Duntz.

Maybe it was time to step it up a notch.

"If you tell us what you know," Taylor said, "we might be able to help you out."

Wesley gave her a look. It was a bit of a risky move, bringing up the charges, but they needed something more.

"We aren't after you, so long as you tell us the truth."

"I am telling the truth," Terrance said.

"You probably think you are," Taylor said, "but it's not adding up." Taylor paused. "Olivia Newman. Zoe Duntz. Do those names mean anything to you?"

Terrance blinked at them with confused, bleary eyes. "No?"

"They were both murdered," Wesley snapped.

Terrance's face went white. "What?"

"Do you know what happens to murderers around here, Terrance?" Wesley said. "They end up on this exact table, in this exact chair, under a bright light, just like you right now. They don't get away with it. Not on our watch."

"What?" Terrance exclaimed. "I'm not a murderer! I have no idea

60

what you're talking about. I don't know those women."

Taylor's eyes hardened. She learned in and said, "Where were you two nights ago?"

"I was working! The graveyard shift, man!"

"Can anyone confirm that?" said Wesley.

"You can ask my boss! I was there all night."

"And where were you the night before?"

"I was at a friend's house. We got high."

"Can anyone confirm that?"

"A few people. I don't remember who, exactly."

Wesley slammed a fist on the table. The interrogation room echoed with the noise, making Taylor wince.

"If you don't tell us the truth, Terrance, then this will be a lot harder for you."

Terrance blinked at them. "Why are you doing this to me? I've done nothing wrong."

Wesley leaned forward. "You've done plenty wrong, Terrance."

"But I didn't kill anyone!" Terrance said.

Wesley grabbed him then, by the collar and yanked him forward. "You love chasing after women, don't you, Terrance? They're like little trophies to you, aren't they? You get off on it. There was a witness that saw you leaving the scene of Olivia Newman's death. And you were seen leaving the scene of Zoe Duntz's death, too. So you're going to talk, Terrance."

"But I didn't do it!" Terrance exclaimed, tears welling in his eyes.

"Then who did?" Wesley asked, relaxing back into his chair. It was all part of his play.

Terrance straightened up. "I don't know."

Truthfully, Taylor wasn't convinced Terrance was their guy. She also didn't think Wesley's aggressive approach was getting them anywhere; all he was doing was scaring the perp. She gently touched his arm, hoping he'd take the signal. Wesley eyed her, but took a breath and relaxed in his seat, letting her take over.

"We're just asking questions, Terrance," Taylor said. She took out her phone and opened up the evidence photos of the ghost orchids. "Does this flower mean anything to you?" She showed him the photos. Terrance's brows pinched as he observed them.

"What the... it looks like a ghost orchid, but..."

Taylor perked up. "But what?"

"But something's not right. It looks tampered with." Terrance paused, and Taylor's heart raced. "That's not even a real ghost orchid. It looks like someone painted it to look like one."

Taylor and Wesley exchanged a confused look.

"You're serious?" Taylor asked.

"Yeah, man, but I don't know—what does this have to do with me being a murderer?"

Taylor abruptly stood. If Terrance was right, then that would completely change the game. "Stay here," Taylor told him.

Wesley stood up too and eyed Terrance. "We'll confirm that alibi. Don't you move a muscle."

With that, Taylor and Wesley breezed out of the interrogation room.

Wesley shook his head as they walked. "That guy seems like a real weirdo."

"Yeah, he does," Taylor said, "but he might just be telling the truth."

Taylor picked up her pace, navigating her way through headquarters. She needed to get to evidence and confirm if the ghost orchid really was a fake. Her blood was up now; she knew the case was close to cracking. She felt it.

The evidence room was at the end of a hallway, guarded by security. Taylor and Wesley were quickly admitted. Inside, it was dark and silent, save for the humming lights above them. Taylor's footsteps echoed on the tiled floor. Even deeper, it became a large, well organized room.

The evidence technician was a woman named Sarah, who was just getting off work. She was a short, round woman in her thirties, who had a kind voice and soft blue eyes. Sarah was on her computer as they approached. She looked up when she saw them. "Hey," she said.

Taylor said, "Hey, Sarah, have you dealt with the murder cases that came in before? The ones with the ghost orchids?"

"I have," Sarah said. "They're in the back."

"Can we look over them?"

"Sure."

Sarah led them behind the counter and pointed to the gray lockers that lined the wall. There were metal shelves up to the ceiling, filled with evidence from investigations. Taylor cruised past the row of desks and grabbed a pair of latex gloves from the dispenser. Wesley was looking a little bemused by the whole process. Meanwhile, Taylor's stomach was in knots. The ghost orchids recovered at the scenes were too delicate to touch, and had remained in the back, safely locked away. Sarah went into another room, then came back out with one of the orchids, contained safely in a box.

Sarah placed the box on a table. Both Taylor and Wesley leaned over to get a closer look.

"What are you hoping to see, Sage?" Wesley asked.

Taylor squinted as she observed the flower closer.

Sure enough, on the petal, was a tiny speck of chipped paint.

"They are fake," Taylor said.

Wesley put his hand on his forehead. "Shit. We've been chasing our tails this whole time."

Taylor's heart raced. This changed everything. They'd been hunting down an expert botanist—but he was nothing but a fraud. Which meant the entire profile of the killer needed to be re-examined.

Maybe it wasn't such a bad thing, though. In fact, this clue could be everything—but Taylor wanted to build up the profile more, and she wanted to do it quickly. Right now. Before another body dropped.

And sometimes, it didn't hurt to seek outside help. There was a BAU agent stationed right in the building, one who Taylor had heard glowing reviews about.

It was time to pay her a visit.

CHAPTER THIRTEEN

Taylor walked into the BAU unit at Quantico with Wesley at her side, feeling a steely determination wash over her. This new information was huge. Taylor couldn't help but feel like this was the biggest clue they'd found yet, like it could bring them right to the killer's door.

In the hallway, Taylor knocked on a door with a name on it: BAU Agent Millie Evans.

"Come in," the voice inside called, and Taylor pushed the door open, her chest full of nerves.

Agent Millie Evans was typing away at her computer. She was an older woman, probably in her late fifties. Her hair was tucked up in a bun and she wore glasses. She looked up with a smile and set her hands on the desk.

"Chief Winchester told me you were on your way. Nice to meet you, Special Agent Sage," she said, holding out a hand. "And you as well, Special Agent Wesley."

Taylor shook her hand and sank down into a chair. "Likewise."

Wesley did the same, and Millie's warm eyes fell on Taylor.

"I read your profile for the Jeremiah Swanson killings," Millie said. "It's pretty thorough. Very impressive. I'm not sure you need me, but I'm happy to help."

Taylor felt her cheeks flush. She didn't like to be complimented, but it was nice to hear her reputation had spread throughout HQ. That meant she was doing a good job. "Thank you. I figured the faster we can work this thing out, the better, so if you have time to help, that would be invaluable."

"Of course, I'll do whatever I can. So, where do we start?" Millie asked, eyes flicking back and forth between Taylor and Wesley.

"We're hoping to build a profile of the killer based on the evidence we have so far," Taylor told her. "We just made a major breakthrough. The killer had been leaving ghost orchids at the crime scenes, which initially made us believe he was an extremely talented botanist capable of growing and keeping such a rare and delicate flower. But it turns out they aren't ghost orchids at all—they're fakes."

Millie raised her eyebrows. "Fakes?"

64

"Yes," Taylor said. "They were painted to look like ghost orchids. But they're just regular orchids."

"Right. So what's the motive for that?" Wesley asked. "Why would the killer go to all the trouble to do that?"

"And what does it say about the killer?" Taylor added. "This is the one thing that we still haven't been able to figure out—what his motive is."

"We think it's a male, and he's most likely in his mid-thirties," Wesley said.

Taylor added, "And the killer is not only educated and knowledgeable, but he also has access to a greenhouse; and he's meticulous enough to make these orchids as close to the real thing as possible and then bring them to the crime scenes."

Millie paused, blinking for a moment. "Wow, aren't you two in sync? Chief Winchester mentioned you'd just started working together. I'd never guess."

Taylor felt heat rise to her cheeks. Wesley was proving to be an excellent partner. And with the way he handled her near-death situation earlier, she'd gained respect for him. Even if his methods could be more aggressive than she liked to be.

When neither Taylor nor Wesley replied, Millie went on.

"Okay. So tell me about the victims. Let's start there, and I'll see if I can help you brainstorm."

Taylor nodded. "First, we have Olivia Newman, a small-time, up and coming actress. Then, Zoe Duntz, a social media star with ten million followers."

"Wow," Millie said. "So one was almost famous, and one was famous. That seems significant."

"We thought so too," Wesley said.

Taylor thought back on the two victims. What did they have in common, other than the "fame" aspect? The story that Zoe's parents told her flared in her mind. How Zoe had some fans who were angry with her for Photoshopping her social media pictures.

And then Olivia. Her fans didn't seem "angry" with her. But...

She had altered herself too, but in real life. She'd had a nose job.

The realization hit Taylor like a tidal wave. The fake images on social media, the fake image in real life.

The fake ghost orchids.

It all had to be connected.

"Special Agent Sage," Millie's soothing voice said. "You seem like you just had a realization."

"Oh, I did." Taylor leaned forward. "I think we know what the victims' connection is. Olivia had plastic surgery, while Zoe altered her photos. The ghost orchid itself was a fake."

Millie leaned back and crossed her arms, thinking. "The ghost orchid... it's symbolic."

"More than that," Wesley cut in, looking Taylor in the eyes like he was having the same epiphany as her. "It's a statement," Wesley said.

"It's a way of saying they were fake," Taylor said. "Like they don't deserve to be taken seriously. These women changed the way they looked. Both of them. Zoe through editing, Olivia through surgery."

"Yes," Millie said, her eyes alight with excitement. "It's a message. He's telling us he doesn't like it. He doesn't think they should have changed the way they looked."

"Exactly," Taylor said. "Which means the killer is not only angry at these two women, he's lashing out at the entire celebrity culture. Not just the people at the top, but all of them. Everyone who thinks that fame, popularity, or money are important."

"The killer probably does, too," Millie said. "What about his identity? Do you have any theories about that?"

"We think he's white, and educated," Taylor explained. "Someone who is upset with the society he lives in."

"With all of that in mind," Millie said, "I think we have a profile now. A man, angry and bitter at the world of beauty."

"He hates people who are 'fake,'" Taylor concluded. "He must spend a lot of time on the internet. I'd guess mid-twenties to mid-thirties."

"So what does his 'statement' mean?" Wesley asked.

"I think it's about pretending to be something you're not," Taylor said.

They all went silent for a moment, considering this. Taylor envisioned the man, who she could only picture as bitter and resentful. Envious. A thief of life and beauty.

They had a general profile now—but she still had no idea where to actually go from there.

Taylor and Wesley stood, realizing they were taking up too much of Millie's time.

But Millie just smiled, shaking her head.

"I'm just glad to be helpful to you. Take care of yourselves, and each other," Millie said, standing.

She walked them to the door and Taylor shook her hand again.

With that, Taylor and Wesley went into the hallway. They stopped and faced each other. Wesley towered over Taylor, and she looked up at him, trying to read where his head was at. But she still didn't know him well enough to figure him out.

"We worked good together in there," Wesley said.

Taylor hadn't expected that, but she couldn't agree more; like Millie said, they'd been in sync. "Thanks. I think so too."

"I'm not one to give praise. But you're a strong thinker, Sage."

Taylor clammed up under the compliment, simply nodding. "It's not quite enough, though," she said. "We still need more data."

"Agreed." Wesley checked his watch. "But let's break for tonight, reconvene in the a.m."

"You sure? I have more left in me."

Wesley smiled a bit. "I can tell. But I need to get home."

Taylor wondered what "home" was to him. But she wasn't about to fight him on it; if he had places to be, then Taylor could continue this on her own. "I'll keep brainstorming," she told him.

"You do that, Sage," Wesley said. "If anything comes up, call me."

Taylor nodded and he left, heading back to his office. She walked down the hall, feeling a rush inside. Somehow, despite his gruffness, Wesley was beginning to grow on her.

But before she could get too excited, she caught herself. They'd learned too much today for Taylor to just stop. She had every intention of continuing her work, and she considered staying here at Quantico. But Taylor had a home to get back to as well.

Even if there was no longer any part of what makes a "home" left in it.

***

Taylor returned to a quiet, dark, and empty house. She thought to herself that she'd never get used to walking through the door and not feeling Ben's warmth or smelling his cooking. Everything was collecting dust; even the few memories they'd made in this place.

Her stomach rumbled with hunger, and exhaustion weighed her down. She had nearly died today, and the weight of it hadn't hit her until she walked through the door, wishing for some at-home comfort that no longer existed.

He should be here, she thought, a bubble of anger growing in her. Taylor was pissed with Ben for leaving her like that. Some days, she even hated him.

But the good memories still crept into her mind, tainting her. She could never forget the reason she'd married him in the first place. Their future had seemed so bright...

Taylor wondered: Was Ben as disappointed as she was, or was he grateful that things were rocky? Had he grown sick of her?

When Taylor thought about it, things had been rocky for a long time, before they even moved to Pelican Beach. But they had been rocky in the way that was nearly invisible until now, until Taylor had the hindsight to *see* the issues in the relationship

For one, Ben had been pushy on the whole kids thing. A bit too pushy. And Taylor had been too reluctant. There were two sides to this story, and she knew she wasn't blameless. Her lack of commitment had rightfully bothered him, and he'd been upfront about his desire for kids. Taylor still felt like an asshole for all of that.

But then again, there was the other monster under their bed—the fact that Ben had two faces when it came to Taylor's work.

He would *say* he was fine with her being away from home so much, but then he'd complain about it later. He said he wanted to move to Pelican Beach with her, only to complain about leaving Portland later.

Thinking about all of this frustrated Taylor more. She wanted answers. She wanted to know what he was thinking.

Heaving out a sigh, she sat on the couch, the same couch where she had confessed her infertility to him. Within weeks, he'd left her. As far as she knew, he was still staying with his sister. But they hadn't spoken in days. No more than the odd text message.

You still at your sister's?

Yes.

And that would be about it.

Taylor took out her cell phone and peered at her reflection in the screen. Her black hair was messy, and her gray eyes were tired. She had every intention of going downstairs to keep going with the profile on the case, but she also needed to eat. She glanced into her kitchen, which she could see through the doorway. Dishes were piling up.

Takeout it was.

After ordering Chinese on a delivery app, she considered going downstairs to isolate herself, but something stopped her.

She wanted to know what Ben was doing, what he was thinking. On paper, he was still her husband.

So she called him.

She expected to reach his voicemail, but she was relieved when he picked up. Not relieved because she was happy to talk to him, per se— she was more relieved that she might get a damn answer from his actual mouth, instead of a one-word reply via text.

"Hello?" he said.

"Hey, Ben."

"Taylor." There was no warmth, no love in his tone. But she was used to his coldness at this point. Did it even hurt anymore? She could barely tell.

There was a pause, before she sighed and pressed on. "Are you still with your sister?"

"Yeah, I am."

"Do you think you'll come back home any time soon?" She felt silly for asking, but she couldn't stop. She needed to know. "Because, I just don't know what I'm going to do about this house and if you want a—"

"I'm not going to come home," Ben said, cutting Taylor off.

Taylor froze. "What?"

Maybe that was an expected outcome. But he was still so cold. So harsh.

He let out a sigh. A woman's voice sounded in the background. "Look, I'm... busy."

Taylor's heart sank into the pits of her stomach. That had to be his sister—right? But Taylor knew Janie's voice, and that sounded way lighter.

They were fighting. Maybe even breaking up. Taylor knew all that. But they were still married.

He wouldn't do this... it can't be... Taylor could barely bring herself to think it.

"Ben," Taylor said, her voice even, "you are aware we're still married."

"Only on paper, Taylor," he said softly.

Taylor couldn't believe it. What did that mean? That he was free to see other people?

Was *this* the man she'd married?

She had spent so much time thinking about the good memories. But maybe those were the fakes ones. Maybe this cold, callous, indifferent person was the real Ben Chambers. And she'd just been fooled. Fooled, the same way the killer had fooled her with those fake ghost orchids.

"Ben, who is it?" that woman's voice called in the background of the call. Taylor could hear it clearer now.

It was definitely not his sister.

Taylor's hands shook. Anger took over the hurt. It came in through a set of floodgates.

He was seeing someone else.

Maybe he'd already slept with her.

The thought made Taylor's blood burn hotter than magma. She couldn't think, couldn't see past the red.

"Go fuck yourself," she said, before she hung up.

Shaking, Taylor stared at her phone, her stomach turning over and over. She felt like she was going to throw up.

Taylor sat there on the couch and buried her face in her hands. She had never spoken to Ben that way. Shame tore her apart. She had become so pathetic in this whole ordeal. Taylor had tried to get him back, to get back what she had lost, but now she knew that she wouldn't.

She would never have him back.

Taylor's breathing was heavy now, and she felt light-headed. She needed to sit down, or even lie down. But her mind wouldn't let her.

Her chest was tight, her hands were shaking.

No. She couldn't let this Ben situation destroy her.

She was an FBI agent. She saved lives for a living.

One man couldn't destroy her resolve—not anymore. She was done letting this situation control her. She needed to go to work, and then she would get her shit together.

Suddenly, the doorbell rang and snapped Taylor out of it.

With a sigh, she did something she hadn't done in a long time: she answered the door. A delivery girl stood there with a plastic bag in her hands. Cold, nighttime air flowed into her house. Feeling numb, Taylor paid the delivery driver and thanked her. She opened the bag to peek inside. Maybe the food was cold. Maybe the chill would numb her thoughts. It was the best she could hope for.

Taylor ate alone at her dinner table, staring at the space Ben once occupied. She picked at her food and eventually starting poking at the Cantonese noodles. It was no longer weird to eat alone. She was getting used to it.

There was no coming back from this. She was determined not to cry over something that couldn't be changed. She would not dwell on Ben. Not anymore.

This isn't about him, Taylor said to herself. *It's about you, Taylor. This isn't about the past. This is about the present.*

So Taylor finished her meal, allowed herself to recharge, then went downstairs and got to work. As she got settled into the basement, she couldn't help but think that her husband was never who she thought he was. And the killer—he was targeting young women for concealing who they really were.

Fakes. It all felt eerily connected.

CHAPTER FOURTEEN

He had never seen such a fake, detestable man in his life—and he was in the backseat of his own car. *Filthy animal.*

As the driver glided through the night in his car, he felt his rage boil and bubble at his idiotic passenger, chattering away on his cellphone in the back. He was one of those types: the ones who take their time eating and then take ages to pay the bill. He was never on time for anything, nor did he respect the time of others. He never seemed to get out of work on time. He never seemed to have time to do all the things he promised. He was always busy; but he'd never done anything positive with his life.

A shallow waste of space.

Money isn't everything, you fool.

The driver's hands clenched around the steering wheel as his passenger blabbered on and on...

But a smile curled at the driver's face. Because little did his passenger know—this was going to be the last ride of his life.

"Okay, bro, I'll call you back later," the passenger said into his phone and hung up.

The driver eyed him in the rear-view mirror. His passenger's pudgy face was illuminated by his phone screen as he scrolled. Probably looking at all of those fake females on social media.

"Are you comfortable back there?" the driver asked, his voice pleasant. He needed to keep up appearances, after all, since he'd convinced this fool that he was a real cab driver.

"Huh?" His passenger looked up at him like he was offended the driver dared to speak. "Yeah, it's cool, man..." He paused. "You actually look familiar... you drive for any other companies?"

The driver laughed. "Yeah, I drive for a lot of companies. It's not a bad way to make money."

"That's cool, bro," his passenger said. "I sort of run my own company. It's not a big deal."

The driver said nothing, but his anger stewed. He already knew what kind of liar his passenger was.

In the backseat, his passenger must have noticed that they'd gone off-route. He scowled.

"Where are you going, bro?"

"Don't worry about it." The driver smiled again. "I'm taking the fast way. Trust me."

"Uh, okay..."

But of course, his passenger didn't know he was about to be strangled to death. The driver eyed his ribbon, draped over the seat beside him.

"I'm thinking of going out of town for a little while," the driver said, making conversation to fill the space. "I need to get away."

"Yeah, that's a good idea, bro," his passenger said, nodding. "I'm planning on going to Cabo in a few months. Me and my boys are taking the trip."

The driver cleared his throat. "Oh yeah?"

"Yeah, man, we're gonna get a little sun, hit the clubs." He paused. "You know, it'll be fun."

Listening to this idiot talk was giving the driver a headache. He twisted in his seat and grabbed the ribbon. He wound it around his fingers and then tested it, taking one hand off the wheel and pulling. It was sturdy and tight. It would strangle this idiot to death.

But he had to be careful. He needed a quieter spot.

His passenger was still tapping away on his phone in the back. He didn't notice them roll up behind a building on a quiet, dark street.

The driver grabbed the ribbon. His mouth practically watered. It was time to do the deed.

"Bro?" his passenger asked.

But it was the last thing he said before the driver jumped in the backseat and wrapped the ribbon around his throat.

"What the hell, bro?!" he shouted, trying to pull at the ribbon, but it was too tight. "Get off me!"

"Shut up," the driver said. He pulled the ribbon tighter. He felt his passenger's flesh and bones start to crunch.

"Get off me, bro! I'll kill you," the passenger shouted. He continued to kick and struggle, but the driver held him tightly.

"Shut up and die," the driver said.

There was a grin on his face as he heard his passenger's moans and shouts get weaker. He felt a jolt of pleasure as his passenger stopped moving. His eyes rolled back. He would be asleep now. His body would stop resisting. He would go limp.

The driver felt his passenger's body start to loosen in the backseat.

This was the best part.

The driver felt the warmth of life leave his body as his passenger

73

slipped into unconsciousness. He checked his pulse.

Dead.

Just what he deserved.

CHAPTER FIFTEEN

Taylor chased Angie through a wide and open field, but no matter how hard she tried, she couldn't keep up with her.

Another dream, her mind told her. *It's another dream. Just wake up!*

But no matter how hard Taylor tried, it was like wading through quicksand. She had to catch Angie. She had to try.

"Angie, wait!" Taylor shouted. Surreal images surrounded her in the dream world. Taylor ran as fast as she could, but she couldn't get any closer to her sister. "Why are you doing this to me again!?"

Taylor's foot hit a rock, and she stumbled.

She knew that would happen.

It always did.

She fought the urge to just get up and walk away.

"Angie, please!" she begged. Her voice was hoarse, her throat sore from screaming. "Why are you doing this to me?"

The wind howled. The grass swayed. But it wasn't grass at all—it was something else, something Taylor couldn't comprehend. Angie laughed, and Taylor wanted to cry.

"Please. I don't want to see this anymore. I'm so tired."

Tired?

Tired of what?

Tired of what, Taylor?

Tired of what…?

Taylor knew the answer, even if she didn't want to admit it.

She was tired of losing.

She was tired of being alone.

She was tired of always running.

She couldn't take it anymore…

Taylor awoke with a gasp. The familiar sight of her bedroom ceiling materialized before her. Taylor breathed a sigh of relief. It was all just a dream.

Just a dream, she reminded herself.

"Angie? Why are you doing this to me?" she asked in the darkness. The room was still and quiet; nothing moved except for the shadows. There was nothing there.

Nothing there.

Angie was gone. She was never coming back. Taylor had to accept that. But how could she, when she kept being teased by these dreams? By Belasco's ominous predictions? She didn't *want* to accept it. Maybe if there had ever been any evidence in the case to show what happened to Angie, it would be easier to accept. But there was nothing. No body. Not a drop of blood. Just a missing girl.

The television's glow shone from its position on the dresser. Taylor had fallen asleep with the news on. For a moment, she thought she saw Angie's face in the shadows, but it was just a trick of the light. She closed her eyes and took a deep breath, savoring the scent of fresh, cool air that wafted in through the window.

Her clock on the nightstand read 4:04 a.m.

Last night, after her takeout, Taylor had locked herself in the basement for hours, trying to work angles on the case. She felt fairly confident in the profile she was building of the killer—but not confident on where to begin looking. Maybe they could go back to the botanist angle and see if there was anyone in that world that would fit who Taylor was looking for. But it might be like finding a needle in a haystack. Evil people didn't always wear their demons on their sleeves; they often hid in plain sight and finding a man with a closeted hatred of "fakeness" might not be so simple.

With a heavy sigh, Taylor pulled herself out of bed. Maybe a run would clear her head.

Taylor stepped into her running shoes, grabbed her keys and cell phone, slid into her running jacket, and jogged down the stairs. She had an hour before she needed to leave for work. She could use the time to clear her head and hopefully find some inspiration.

It was still dark outside, and the town was quiet, but Taylor saw a few people milling about on the sidewalk to let their dogs out for early morning pees. She could hear cars and busses in the distance, and the sounds of Pelican Beach slowly waking up. Taylor breathed in the crisp air and started down the street.

The usual route through town was too close to home. Taylor knew she wouldn't be running for long—she would be looking for inspiration, so she didn't want to be trapped in her own head.

But of course, she couldn't forget Angie.

Angie's body was never recovered. Taylor tried not to think about that. But it didn't change the fact that it was true. Still, it was like a knife in her heart. Always taunting her with hope.

Taylor breathed deeply, forcing herself to think about something else. She had always been a runner, and she had learned every path in Pelican Beach.

No matter how hard she tried to stifle them, the "what-ifs" and "maybes" crept back into her mind.

What if Angie was alive?

What if she was being held captive by a madman?

What if she was tortured and about to die?

But none of the what-ifs and maybes made any sense.

They were just that: what-ifs and maybes. They were figments of Taylor's imagination, but they weren't reality.

Taylor ran along the main drag through town, lined with shops and restaurants. On the left was the main street of the boardwalk; to the right was the ocean. Further down was the marina. It was a short drive to the harbor. Taylor generally chose to walk there, where the tourists were thick, and the coffee was hot. She ran along the beach below the boardwalk, which was still deserted. There were no fishermen this early in the morning, and the tourists didn't tend to come out for another hour or so.

She considered going by Belasco's shop but stopped herself. She had already asked so much of the woman, and showing up again, so early in the morning, seemed cruel.

But there was another itch growing in her, one that begged to be scratched.

Maybe if she just looked at the evidence from Angie's case, it would help remind her that Angie was never coming back. It could help stomp down this nuisance she called hope.

Or maybe, it would point her to the truth—that Angie really was out there.

Taylor ran all the way back home, her lungs heaving. Once she got inside, she went into the basement, where she uncovered a box. A box she hadn't opened in years.

It contained everything she'd ever learned about Angie's disappearance. Every newspaper article. Every piece of evidence that was released.

Taylor's fingers combed through the files. She hadn't opened these files for years, but she knew them all by heart. The only thing left in the box was the one thing she couldn't bring herself to look at again.

She reached into the box and pulled out the only item that remained.

Angie's old teddy bear.

It was caked with dust, bits of lint and dirt, but Angie had always loved it. When they were kids, she never went anywhere without it.

There were also photos, police reports, and news clips. Taylor couldn't look at them. She knew what they said. They all said the same thing: no sign of Angie Sage's body. No clues to who took her, or where she went. It was like she'd been abducted by aliens.

The box had everything, but it still didn't have what Taylor was looking for.

It didn't have Angie.

She took a deep breath and rubbed her temples again.

"What am I going to do?"

It was time to stop trying to figure out who the killer could be and start looking for him. Taylor didn't know how she was going to do it, but she had to start somewhere.

On the wall of her basement, she began hanging up all of the evidence to create a board. Maybe if she saw it all laid out like this, she would see something she had somehow never seen before.

She placed a photo of Angie next to her teddy bear, then began to lay out the notes. She organized the files into categories:

Theories on how Angie disappeared,

Theories on who killed Angie.

Theories on possible suspects.

Then she got to work.

She scanned the evidence and the articles, arranging them on the board. She took Polaroids of each article and pinned them up. She took notes and wrote down her thoughts at the bottom of each photograph in her looping scrawl.

It was like Taylor was trapped in a trance as she worked. She hadn't even realized how much time had passed—not until her phone buzzed in her pocket. She gasped in shock. An hour had flown by in a matter of minutes.

And Chief Winchester was calling.

"Chief?" Taylor answered.

"Sage, are you on your way to HQ?"

Taylor hurried up the stairs. "Uh—yes, Chief! I'm on my way."

"Change of plans—I need you to meet Wesley in Pine Point." Winchester paused as Taylor reached the first floor. With bated breath, she anticipated his next words: "There's been another murder."

At this point, Taylor was going to be late. She hurried out to her car and got on the road.

CHAPTER SIXTEEN

Taylor pulled her car up to the street in Pine Point, where the next victim allegedly was. Apparently, the news had garnered an audience—there were bystanders watching in horror, whispering to each other, likely speculating on the scene. This was too public to contain.

Taylor got out of her vehicle. A group of police officers was standing around by caution tape beside a row of commercial buildings. In the middle of them was Wesley. Taylor hurried right up to him.

"What's going on? Where's the crime scene?" she asked.

Wesley nodded toward the building up ahead. Taylor hurried over to the scene, and what she saw made her blood run cold.

A man—no older than thirty—lying with his back flat against the sidewalk.

And he was holding a ghost orchid.

A man? Taylor couldn't believe it—the last two victims had been females. The crimes so far had felt so deliberate, so gendered.

This could change everything.

As she drew closer, she made out the face of the man. He was staring up at the sky, with a look of pure terror on his face. He had a clean-shaven, but bloated face.

And that same ribbon mark that the last two victims had was imprinted on his neck.

He had been strangled to death and left right here.

"Not pretty, is it?" Wesley said.

That was one way to put it. This marked the third murder within three days in Pine Point, an otherwise quiet college town. "Whoever is doing this is tearing this town apart," Taylor said. "Do we know who he is?"

"Not yet."

She took a closer look at the body. He was an attractive young man, but his glassy eyes staring up at the sky were haunting. And the ghost orchid was placed so delicately in his hands. A Rolex watch was strapped on his wrist—that thing must have been worth at least twenty grand, if not more. And yet the killer didn't touch it. That could mean he wasn't interested in money—which could mean he was either rich himself, or just didn't care. Either way, the detail seemed significant.

The victim was wearing a casual suit, dressed nicely, like the last two victims. The biggest difference was, of course, his gender.

"Why did this man get the honor of being left with a ghost orchid?" Wesley asked.

"I'm not sure. I don't think it's logical that it's just random," Taylor said. "And the fact that he just left the Rolex…"

"The guy's not in it for the money," Wesley said.

Taylor nodded. "It's definitely someone with a grudge. Someone who knows exactly what he's doing."

"Yeah," Wesley said. "This guy is really fucking with us. This is gonna create a lot of fear in town. People are already freaking out."

They were. Taylor had noticed on her way through the town that everyone was more on edge than usual—even people who didn't know any of the victims. Everyone was walking around with caution in their eyes. Taylor knew that if this kept up, the town was going to be a powder keg. The walls were going to come tumbling down; someone was going to go on a rampage. And this time, it might not just be fear of the killer—it might be fear for the killer. The killer could be the one to snap first.

Taylor would have to talk to the victim's family, too. That was going to be hard. She knew that families of victims always thought there was something they could have done, something they could have said or done to prevent it. They always thought it was their fault.

Taylor noticed something poking out of his pocket. She snapped on a glove before she pulled it out.

It was a business card.

"Derek White," Taylor said. "Fierce Start-ups." She stood up and flashed the card to Wesley. "If this is him, then he's a CEO of some sort of social media start-up company."

"Successful," Wesley commented. "See anything else?"

Taylor took another look at the victim. His suit was immaculate, his body was in great shape. And his skin was flawless. There wasn't a scratch or a blemish on him. However, Taylor didn't see any obvious signs of plastic surgery.

She lifted his arm, and that's when she saw it: a torn thread.

"Wes," Taylor said. "Take a look at this."

Wesley stepped in to get a closer look. "What is it?" he asked.

She tugged gently at the torn thread on the suit. It looked like it had happened during a struggle—maybe Derek fought back.

"So one of the victim's claws almost got away," Wesley said. "Got away while they were killing him."

80

Taylor nodded. "This person is getting more and more vicious."

"Fearless," Wesley added.

"Right," Taylor agreed. "And he's getting more and more reckless." She paused. "I can't believe one of the victims was a man... it's a complete switch in MO."

She took one last look at the victim, and the ghost orchid.

"I'm really starting to hate this flower," she muttered.

"Me too," Wesley said.

Taylor looked around the scene. It was a great place to dump a body. No one would have seen a thing. The body would have been out of sight with the rows of hedges. The killer would have driven off right away and gotten out of there. Taylor shivered. The idea of getting strangled like that, cold and alone, was terrifying.

She looked up at the sky, watching the sun slowly creep westward. She knew she had to head back to the station to send this off to be analyzed. She also had to get more information to put out on the news. More and more people were going to get flowers. And more and more people were going to die.

And the killer was going to get more and more reckless.

They needed to crack this case. And they needed to do it now.

***

Twenty minutes later, Taylor was in the passenger seat of Wesley's car as they went over the details of the case. They were parked near the crime scene, and the morning sun drifted above the clouds, bleeding in through Wesley's sunroof. Taylor had her laptop out and was going over what they knew of the victim.

"So he was born in Pine Point... lived here his whole life—thirty years..." Taylor said, zoning in on the details. Derek graduated from Pine Point High, went to college in Boston, graduated with a business degree, got a job at a local start-up company, Fierce Start-ups, made his way up the corporate ladder, and became CEO.

"He was the youngest CEO of a social media company to go public," Taylor said.

"Good-looking kid too, before well, today…" Wesley pulled out his phone from his pocket and pulled up a picture.

Taylor looked at the screen: it was Derek White's social media profile picture, showing him in a suit. His hair was black, and he had piercing blue eyes. He certainly was handsome in his prime.

"And he has a wife," Wesley said. "They got married in July."

"How long has he been CEO?" Taylor asked.

"About four years. He started it from the ground up."

"I found out he has no record, too," Taylor said. "None at all. Figures."

"I'll check his schedule," Wesley said. "See who he's been meeting with. Maybe he did something he shouldn't have done."

"That's too easy," Taylor said. "We've gotta dig deeper. The killer is choosing these victims for a reason."

Wesley gave her a look. "What are you thinking?"

Taylor thought on it. In order for Derek to qualify as a victim under the profile they'd been building, there needed to be something "fake" about him. But Taylor failed to see what it was. In his photos, Derek didn't appear to have plastic surgery or anything of the sort. His skin had laugh lines and natural wrinkles that come with age. He had a full head of hair, and it looked like his natural color.

It wasn't like he was a hungry politician or a pastor, and it didn't seem that he was working on a project that would make him a lot of enemies. There weren't even any rumors linking the murder to a potential conspiracy or cover-up. Derek White lived a very ordinary and very boring life.

Right. Unless Derek White was a clone of himself manufactured by the government, there was no reason for Taylor to consider him a victim of the Ghost Orchid Killer.

So what put the target on his back?

She couldn't see it now, but there was one person in Derek's life who knew him better than anyone. Taylor turned to Wesley.

"We better go talk to the wife."

CHAPTER SEVENTEEN

Taylor was vibrating in the passenger seat of Wesley's car the whole drive to the Whites' house. The couple's house was a mile outside Pine Point, at the edge of the woods. It was a large house, with a beautiful garden, and a winding pathway leading to the front door. It was clear that Derek had millions, based on this estate.

Taylor and Wesley got out of the car and walked up the long, cobblestone driveway.

"Nice place," Wesley muttered.

The agents made their way up the pathway, to the front door, which was made from a dark wood with square-shaped windows on it. Very modern, and so different from the colonial-style house Ben had chosen for them in Pelican Beach. The house Taylor now wanted nothing to do with.

Taylor pressed the doorbell. There was a momentary pause, and then she heard footsteps.

She caught a glimpse of Derek's wife through the glass. She was a statuesque blonde woman with blue eyes. A few seconds later, Monica White, a beautiful woman in her late-twenties, opened the door. She was dressed simply, with a plain blue shirt and jeans. Her blonde hair was in a bun, and she had clearly been crying, judging by her red-rimmed eyes. She had just learned her husband had been murdered, after all; Taylor couldn't imagine the pain that she was going through.

It didn't matter what Ben did to her. She never wanted any harm to come to him.

"Monica White?" Taylor asked.

"Hi, that's me," she said, trying to keep it together.

"I'm Special Agent Taylor Sage, and this is my partner, Special Agent Wesley. May we come in?" Taylor said.

Monica hesitated, then opened the door. Taylor and Wesley walked inside. The smell of pine filled the house, and the decorations in the house were both modern and traditional, reflecting the history of Pine Point. The house was open and spacious, with odd-sized windows that let in lots of natural light. Pictures of Monica and Derek were scattered around the living room, and the walls were painted in a soft cream. Plus, with all the plants inside, it felt like the whole room was full of fresh oxygen.

Monica gestured for Taylor and Wesley to sit on their opulent couch in the living room. Taylor accepted the offer, while Wesley leaned against the arm of the couch. He still maintained his tough, distant exterior.

Monica folded her hands as she sat on the loveseat.

"I'm so sorry for your loss," Taylor said.

"It's been terrible. Terrible," Monica said, looking like she was about to cry again. Then she sniffed. "I'm not sure how helpful I could be."

"I understand," Taylor said. "You're going through a lot right now."

"It's a nightmare. Derek's gone. Just like that," Monica said, snapping her fingers.

"I can't imagine how difficult this is," Taylor said. "But I do have a few questions."

Monica nodded, fondling the neck of her blouse.

"What can you tell me about Derek?" Taylor began.

Monica put her hands to her eyes, trying to stop the tears. "Everything. He was... he was the love of my life. We've been together for five years. He was the CEO of a start-up for four years, and... and we got married over the summer."

"He was a big success," Taylor said. "That must have been rewarding."

"It was..." Monica gestured to the beautiful home around them. "He's the reason why we could live like this."

Wesley cut in, "With money like that, Derek must have made some enemies."

Taylor shot Wesley a look. He was being too abrupt, as always.

Monica blinked. "Ah, well... sort of."

Taylor leaned forward, clasping her hands. "Derek had enemies?"

"Well, he'd always maintained good business relationships... until recently."

Taylor exchanged a look with Wesley.

"What happened recently?" Wesley asked.

"He actually was being investigated for lying to his shareholders about profit margins," Monica said. "But—it's not true! Derek wouldn't do that."

Taylor's heart raced. This could be it--the thing that made Derek "fake." The thing that could have put him on the killer's radar.

"Do a lot of people know about this?" Taylor asked.

"It has gotten out," Monica said. "Word spreads quickly in a town

84

like this."

"I bet it does," Taylor said.

Monica's eyes were watery. "This is... all I want is to know the truth. I want to believe that Derek didn't lie to me. That's why I'm here, you know."

"I understand," Taylor said.

Monica played with her collar. "I don't know if you know this, but Derek was good friends with a lot of important people in the town."

"Hm," Taylor said, thinking. She turned to Wesley.

Wesley pulled out his notepad and pen. "These enemies. Who are they?"

"I don't know," Monica said. "It's mostly the shareholders and employees, I guess."

Wesley said, "Derek must have had some kind of motive. He wouldn't just lie to his shareholders without a reason."

"I don't know," Monica said. "Maybe the pressure got to him? I don't know... maybe he did lie, and I was just blinded by love."

"But if he did, who do you think would want to kill him for that?" Taylor asked.

Monica's eyes widened. "But... no one would."

"It could have been anyone," Wesley said.

"No, I don't think that's true," Monica said. "The company's stock is going to plummet with Derek gone. Everyone was mad at him, but to kill him over it--that would just cost them money."

Taylor understood where Monica was coming from, and it was doubtful that the Ghost Orchid Killer was a shareholder in Derek's company.

Still, it was worth looking into. This was a strong lead.

"Monica, do you mind if I see Derek's office?" Taylor asked.

"Not at all. I would be glad to show you."

The two agents followed Derek's wife up the winding staircase in the back of the house, heading to the second floor. The hardwood floors on the second floor were covered with a tan carpet, and there was a beautiful photograph of the ocean hanging on the wall.

They made their way to a room to the right. Derek's home office was dark compared to the rest of the house. The walls were lined with bookshelves, and there was a large oak desk in front of the window. The room was painted a deep, dark red that contrasted the cream and white of the rest of the house. All in all, it felt very manly. A place where Derek could get away from it all and get down to business.

Taylor didn't know what she was looking for, but she wanted to get a stronger sense of Derek.

She scoured the surface of his desk for clues. He had a few framed pictures of him with his wife and a photo of him with a group of men, probably his employees. He was smiling in all of them. She glanced in the drawers of his desk, but there were mostly papers and office supplies.

There was a pair of glasses, a half-full mug of coffee, a penholder with a few pens, a few stacks of paper and an old-fashioned Rolodex with cards in it. Judging from the size of the Rolodex, the business must have had a lot of important contacts.

Taylor flipped open a book, only to realize a pen was on a specific page.

And on the page, it read: DEAL WITH KALL.

"Who's Kall?" Taylor asked.

***

"This is it," Wesley said, parking the car. Taylor could get used to the chauffer service. She climbed out of Wesley's car and walked to the front of the Fierce Start-ups building. The company had only gotten out of beta two years ago and was trying to make itself into a major player in the social media industry. They were trying to gain a foothold in the market, and were clearly doing pretty well for themselves, considering they were still in their infant stages.

"We'd better get some answers here," Wesley muttered. "I'm sick of the dead ends."

"We don't have a subpoena," Taylor said, approaching the front door.

"Yeah, and we don't have time for one either," Wesley said.

It was true; it could take hours to get approved, but Taylor wanted to get into Derek's work ASAP and find some answers.

"Either way," Taylor said, "I'd like to have a word with whoever Kall is."

The building was a simple cube made of concrete and glass. It was three stories high and had about a dozen windows. The company was trying to create a work environment that looked like a "social hub," so they'd put in lots of glass and bright neon lights. The entire building was plastered with colorful posters and slogans. The agents went inside and were greeted by a pleasant smell of burning candles.

Taylor and Wesley went up to the front desk, where a pretty brunette was sitting. She had a name tag that said "Missy."

"Can I help you?" she asked sweetly.

"We wanted to ask a few questions about Derek White," Taylor said, showing her badge.

"Oh, I heard what happened to him," Missy said. "It's so awful."

"Did you know Derek?" Taylor asked.

Missy was quiet for a moment. "Of course, everyone knew Derek."

"Was he a bit of a slimy guy?" Wesley cut in. Harsh, as always. It wasn't Taylor's style, but she had to admit: Wesley got people talking.

"Well..." Missy looked over her shoulder, then back at the agents. "I don't think so. Derek was really nice to me. But we all know the rumors..."

"About him lying to shareholders and investors," Taylor clarified.

Missy nodded.

"I didn't believe the rumors," Missy said. "I mean, I still don't think he'd actually do it. But it's strange, isn't it? He was a really nice guy. It doesn't make any sense that he'd do that."

"Any strange visitors you can think of?" Taylor asked.

"No one in particular... but I mean, I don't know the whole staff very well. It's hard to know everyone when you're behind the front desk the whole time."

"Thanks. And one more question: Does the name Kall mean anything to you? Is there anyone here who works here by that name?"

"Um, no, but let me check..." Missy went onto her computer. "No, sorry. No Kall."

"Thanks, Missy," Taylor said. Missy was clearly eager to help, so Taylor risked a braver question: "Is there any way you can give us a name of investors and shareholders in the company?"

Missy's eyes went wide. "Oh, my, no, I can't do that."

"We're with the FBI," Wesley said, his voice hard. "We would greatly appreciate your cooperation." But it sounded more like a threat.

"I'll looe my job," Missy scrambled. "Our shareholders are strictly confidential. You guys need a subpoena, or else I'll get fired."

Of course, Taylor had already predicted that; it was easy to learn who worked there, but who was actually invested was pretty confidential, for obvious reasons.

Wesley's tanned cheeks reddened, and Taylor could tell this was frustrating him. It frustrated her, too—there was a killer on the loose, and even for the FBI, getting a subpoena could take serious time.

But there was nothing they could do; Taylor couldn't force this girl to sacrifice her job.

"We'll get on that, then," Taylor said. "Thank you."

Taylor and Wesley walked out of the building. They climbed back into Wesley's car but were silent. Taylor couldn't tell what Wesley was thinking.

"I'll call and get the subpoena," he said. "Could take hours, though." Frustrated, Wesley punched the steering wheel. Taylor flinched.

"Jesus, Wesley," Taylor said, suddenly fuming. She hated when men got unnecessarily violent.

Taking a deep, shaky breath, he calmed down. "I apologize, Special Agent Sage. But I'm frustrated."

"I am too. We don't need to punch things." Taylor put her hands to her temples. The headache was starting to come on again.

Wesley sighed. "I'm sorry."

Taylor decided to be mature. "That's okay."

A few seconds of silence passed before Wesley said, "You know, Monica White's reaction didn't seem suspicious to you?"

Taylor thought on it. Monica didn't seem suspicious to her. "She seemed like she was in shock."

"That's what I mean. She didn't seem heartbroken."

Taylor looked away from Wesley. "Well, people deal with grief differently. I thought she seemed pretty upset."

"Yeah." Wesley paused, ran his hand along his chin, which had a five o'clock shadow. "I'm looking too deep into things. We need that subpoena."

Taylor checked her watch. "Call it in, then let's break for lunch."

"Okay." He paused. "I'll drop you off at your car."

She meant to imply that Wesley could come with her, and they could get some one-on-one time to know each other more—but he didn't seem interested. He was clearly the loner type, so Taylor didn't take it personally.

Besides, Pine Point was a lot closer to Baltimore than Pelican Beach—she could get her dad to meet her halfway and have lunch with him.

There was no one better she could think of to help go over the psych profile of the killer.

CHAPTER EIGHTEEN

"My baby!" Taylor's dad, Randall, exclaimed, his deep voice booming. He was waiting for her when she got to the diner. He had on a gray suit with a black tie and his wavy, white hair was perfectly coiffed. Taylor was always happy to see him, like she was back home again, no matter where they were. He wore thin-rimmed glasses and greeted Taylor with a kiss to her cheek. She was lucky he was available—he had a really busy practice and was often tied up with patients during the day.

Taylor smiled. She was used to her dad's outbursts. "Hi, Dad."

They sat at a booth, and Taylor ordered a black coffee with a burger, and her dad got the same. As the waitress walked away, Taylor met her dad's eyes, reminded briefly of Angie—and her obsessive thinking the other day. She didn't want her dad to know that she was back to her same old ways, obsessing over her sister's disappearance again. It concerned him, and Taylor had already heard the lectures before.

"You must be working on a big case," her dad said. "I was wondering if it had anything to do with those ghost orchid killings I've been seeing on the news. You mentioned Pine Point, so I put two and two together…"

Taylor's dad knew her well, so it was no surprise he already knew exactly what they were working on. She didn't see any reason to lie to him—he was a professional. "Yeah, we've got that case. It's pretty bizarre, actually."

"I know," he said. "There's been a lot of news coverage. We're even hearing about it in Baltimore. It seems like a tough nut to crack."

Taylor nodded. "Well, you know how much I love puzzles."

"I know," he said. "I remember when you were little, and you used to look for clues in the house. You were always fascinated by those old mystery books."

"How do you know I was little? I could have been five," she countered.

"Oh, I don't know… I guess I always just remember you as a little girl."

Taylor thought back. Her childhood was a happy, yet painful time.

Happy because Angie was still around, and she had two loving parents, something not everyone had. But sad because it was all in the past now, so distant, so far away.

She felt bad for not telling her dad what was going on with Ben. It was shameful for her to lie to her father, who had always encouraged honesty from her; but Taylor just wasn't ready to talk about the whole situation. He'd find out soon eventually, but for now, she had called him here for a reason.

"Anyway, I didn't want to meet up to walk down memory lane, sadly," Taylor said.

Her dad smiled. "You never do, sweetheart. How can I help?"

"I was hoping you could help me build a more detailed profile of the killer."

They paused as the waitress placed their plates in front of them before she zipped away. Taylor's dad immediately popped a fry in his mouth. "What do you have so far?"

"Well, for one," Taylor said, dipping a fry in ketchup, "the ghost orchids left at the crime scenes are fakes. He painted and trimmed regular orchids to look just like them. That's not on the news yet."

"An impressive attention to detail," her dad said. He moved onto his burger and took a bite. Taylor did the same, but she was more concerned about talking her dad's ear off than eating.

"Yes," she said, putting her food down. "Furthermore, we have three victims so far—each of them has been accused of being 'fake' in some way. The first had plastic surgery. The second used Photoshop. And the third was caught lying to shareholders."

Her dad leaned back in his seat, running a hand along his chin. Taylor was very curious to know what kind of profile he would build based on that information.

"The first thing that comes to mind is that he is likely male," he said. "I think, based on that, that we're dealing with someone who is insecure. They're constantly doubting themselves and their abilities, and they're probably very sensitive. Their friends or family might have said something that made them feel like they were a fake—and since they're so insecure, they decided to take revenge on these people who they thought were also fakes."

Taylor smiled. Her dad never disappointed. "That's exactly it," Taylor said. "I think the fake ghost orchids are a statement."

"They're beautiful, but fake... I suppose it's a way for him to say these people didn't deserve to live. I wonder what happened in his childhood—or adult life—that would trigger him to do this."

"Any ideas?" Taylor asked.

"Well, it's hard to say," her dad said, his eyes growing distant. "It might be a result of some kind of abuse or neglect—the killer might have been shamed or humiliated by someone they cared about. But they were powerless to stop it. They're probably trying to live up to the expectations of their parents. They're trying to be perfect, and they feel like they're never good enough. But obviously, they're still clever enough to kill people and get away with it for this long." Her dad paused. "I do sense a component of rage here as well, though."

"That's what I was thinking before too," Taylor said. "I feel like he's angry with the people he kills for being 'fake.'"

"That's the rage talking," her dad said. "They're probably not even that fake... just come close to it in his eyes. Something could have happened in his childhood that made him focus on the concept of 'fake' and what it means to him."

"Like what?"

"Well, if he was neglected, perhaps he was forced to take care of himself. He could have had to cook his own meals, do his own laundry, that kind of thing. His parents might have been more concerned with their own problems than taking care of him. He could have even been physically or emotionally abused, and the parent didn't do anything about it. If he was angry about that, he might have turned on the parent, blaming them for the abuse, saying that they were too fake to help him."

Taylor sighed. "So what you're saying is that sometimes, you have to look at the situation before you can figure out the motive."

"Yes. It's the motive that leads you to the killer, not the other way around."

"Thanks, Dad. That was really helpful. I feel like I'm finally getting somewhere with this case." Taylor took a breath. This was a pretty good profile. "So we're looking for an insecure, sensitive male, who lost their temper and killed their victims because they thought their victims were fakes."

"Sounds about right." Her dad looked her over. "Any suspects?"

"Not yet. But I'm hoping we can get someone soon."

"Good luck, sweetheart. Keep me posted."

A pause hung in the air they both poked at their food. But then Taylor noticed her dad studying her.

"What is it?" she asked.

"Nothing, you just look tired," her dad said. "I'd like to see you take some time off, you know. You're working too hard. If you're in this deep, we should be meeting up more often."

Taylor kind of agreed, but she had a bad habit of working too hard. It was what made her who she was. Bury all of her emotions under layers and layers of work. "Okay, Dad. Maybe when this case is over."

"Deal." Her dad finished his burger, and Taylor did the same.

"How's Ben?" her dad asked, fixing his napkin.

Taylor froze. She'd been praying this wouldn't come up. "He's... good," Taylor said, hoping her dad wouldn't catch her in a lie.

A flash of concern crossed her dad's face. "Something's been going on for a while," her dad said. "You can tell me, sweetheart. I won't judge."

Taylor clammed up. She didn't want to tell him this, not here, not now. "Soon, Dad," she mumbled. "I promise. Just let me figure it out on my own first, okay?"

He smiled. "Of course. I trust you."

Suddenly, Taylor's phone buzzed in her pocket. "Sorry, Dad, I have to take this."

It was Wesley. Taylor answered quickly.

"Wes, what's going on?"

"Sage, I need you to meet me at HQ," he said. "I think we've got something." A pause. "Derek was keeping more from his wife than investment fraud."

***

Taylor hurried into the Quantico briefing room, where Wesley was waiting. He stood above the table, leaning over it so he could scroll through his laptop, and didn't even look up as Taylor entered. It looked like he'd spent the whole lunch hour working without her, and Taylor felt a tinge of annoyance; if Wesley had communicated, she would've gladly skipped lunch to keep running things down. It wasn't like she'd spent any of her lunch thinking about much other than work.

"Did you get the subpoena?" Taylor asked.

"Not yet," Wesley muttered.

"Oh," Taylor said. "Then why—"

"Look at this."

Taylor came over to the laptop and peered at the screen. On it was a series of emails--sent directly to Derek White.

"You got into his email," Taylor said.

As much as Taylor understood what it was like to want to work alone, she couldn't help but feel annoyed. She would've worked this angle with Wesley if he'd let her know. Partnership was supposed to be about teamwork. She made a mental note to talk to him about it later—again—but for now, she needed to focus on the case. They could work out the kinks in their partnership soon; this was all still new territory. For both of them.

Leaning closer to the laptop, Taylor read the emails on the screen. The emails were all nasty and directed at Derek.

You're a scumbag, Derek White, a lying scumbag! The world will see you for who you are.

And:

You're lucky we don't hang you for what you did!

"Looks like someone was sending him death threats," Taylor said.

The first few were simple, coded death threats--messages about how Derek was going to die, how his life was going to be destroyed, and how all of it was "all his fault."

Every email was written by a different person--the first three were all sent by "R@nk," and then another was sent by "A@rrow," and then another was sent by "K@ll."

Taylor's pulse jumped. K@ll--that could be Kall, the person in Derek had referred to. "Kall," she said.

"Exactly," said Wesley. "The phrasing of the first three matches, but then someone else came along and sent an email with a different phrasing."

Taylor's brow furrowed. "A different phrasing?"

"Yeah," Wesley said. "Take a look."

Taylor read the email sent by "K@ll"—AKA Kall.

"I'm going to hunt you down," she read, "and I'm going to kill you." Taylor shivered. "We better get an IP on this one."

"Already on it."

Wesley pulled up a new window, where he had already traced the IP—leading right to a house in Pine Point.

"His name is Simon Gibbons," Wesley said. "And he's a horticulturist."

CHAPTER NINETEEN

As Taylor walked up the driveway of Simon Gibbons's house, Wesley beside her, she was ready to take this guy down. Simon Gibbons lived in a small, white-sided house right on the waterfront, with a small garden in the front yard. It was colorful, with roses and tulips of all kinds blooming.

Beautiful place for a potential killer to live.

Taylor knocked on the door. "Mr. Gibbons," she called, "this is Special Agent Taylor Sage from the FBI. I'd like to ask you some questions about the emails you sent to Derek White."

No answer came.

Wesley knocked on the door this time, his massive fist sending sound waves through the whole house.

Still no answer.

Taylor looked around the property—there was also no car in the driveway. "He's not here," she concluded.

Wesley glanced down at her. "Good thing we have a warrant," he said. Given the circumstances, getting one had been no problem. Then, Wesley said: "Stand back, Sage."

"What are you—"

Wesley's massive frame slammed against the door. Once, twice, until it busted right open. Taylor flinched at the ear-shattering sounds.

A little much. But hey, at least he got results.

They stepped inside the house. The first room they came to was the foyer. It was filled with flowers, and the windowsills were lined with potted orchids. The ceiling was covered with vines, a little worse for wear.

"This guy's a little obsessed with flowers," Wesley observed.

"Yeah," Taylor agreed, "but that's not the weird part. Look at the walls."

They were painted a deep purple. It looked like someone had taken a whole can of spray paint and just went to town on the walls. The house had looked beautiful from the outside, but inside—it was bizarre.

"I'll be right back," Wesley said. "Think I'll check the hallway."

He went out of the room, leaving Taylor alone. She waited,

listening to the sound of her own footsteps against the carpet. The walls were covered with pictures, each with some evidence of flowers, but different from the others; the first was an orchid, but the second was a bunch of roses, and the third showed a hydrangea.

They canvassed the home, which turned out to be fairly small—but still, there were dozens of places to look. But Wesley didn't seem bothered—he kept searching, looking at each room carefully and then moving on. Taylor focused on her own search and broke apart from Wesley.

The living room was a mess—literally. The number of flower-related items that were in the room was remarkable, but it was also obvious that whoever lived here didn't give a damn about keeping their house neat. It was filled with dirty dishes and messy shelves, with pots and pans and plates on the kitchen counter, and garbage spilling out of the trash can.

Taylor walked into the kitchen, looked around. It was messy, but nothing else was out of place, nothing seemed to be missing.

Suddenly, her train of thought was interrupted by a small noise.

She froze.

It sounded like a door slamming shut.

Her heart starting racing—had he found the suspect?—and she dashed toward the hallway. She found the bathroom door closed shut.

"Wesley!" she called, and she was immediately met with silence. She took a deep breath, and then she opened the door.

"What—" she began, her voice trailing off as she saw what was inside.

Wesley was standing there, unharmed, flipping through a crossword puzzle booklet. He held it up. "Nothing in here either."

Taylor let out a breath.

"What has you so wound up?" Wesley asked. He walked toward her, his hulking frame nearly touching the ceiling. Taylor felt cornered, so she jumped away from the bathroom's doorway and back into the hall.

"Sorry. I thought I heard something."

She was also used to things going horribly wrong during searches, so she'd had a moment of panic. Not a big deal.

"I'm not seeing anything too suspicious," Wesley said.

"Let's check the bedroom," Taylor said.

The master bedroom was in the back of the house, and it was tiny. Wesley and Taylor walked in. The bed was messy, and there was a closet with a bunch of clothes on the floor. The door was open.

"I'll check that," Wesley said, heading toward the closet. "You check under the bed."

Taylor rolled her eyes—Wesley could be a bit of a control freak sometimes. Not that she could really comment on that; she liked taking the lead herself, and Wesley had been letting her do so. She went to look under the bed. It was fairly large—it could hold two people, if they didn't mind being intimate.

She pulled open the dust ruffle. Nothing.

Then, she stood back up.

And right there was Simon Gibbons. A pair of scissors was in his hand, and he was holding them at Wesley's throat.

"One more step," he said, "and I'll cut his jugular."

Taylor's stomach twisted. They hadn't even heard him come in. This was a huge oversight.

"Simon," Wesley said calmly, "we're looking for you. You're under arrest."

"I don't think so. You're intruders. You're trying to rob me." He was a tall, lanky man with buggy blue eyes, mid-forties. *Damn it.* The last thing Taylor needed was her new partner dead. Wesley was a giant of a man, but Simon had managed to sneak up on him.

"No, Simon, we're with the FBI," Taylor said. She held her hands up in peace. "Please lower the weapon."

Jittery, Simon's eyes darted across the room.

"I don't think you're listening, Simon," Wesley said calmly. "Lower the weapon."

"No way," Simon replied.

And he lifted the scissors as if he were about to stab Wesley right in the throat.

Taylor gasped. Wesley's reaction was immediate—he raised his arm and blocked the attack. The scissors cut into his arm, but instead of crying out, he only grunted. He pushed Simon away with all his might, sending him hurling backwards—but Simon was able to find his footing fast.

"Son of a bitch," Wesley said. He went to pull out his gun, but there was no time—Simon darted at Wesley again with the scissors.

He started to slash at Wesley again, but Taylor couldn't stand to watch it happen. She launched herself at Simon, tackling him to the ground.

Simon hit the floor with a thud, and the scissors fell out of his hand. Taylor covered Simon's body with her own, pinning his arms to his sides. Wesley reached down, picked up the scissors, and then stepped back.

"Get off me," Simon said. He didn't move much—just enough to look up at Taylor with pleading eyes. "Don't take my flowers away," he said.

"Wesley, get my handcuffs," she grunted.

She held Simon down, and Wesley stepped over Simon's head and bent down to pick up the pair of handcuffs out of Taylor's pocket. Taylor snapped the handcuffs on his wrists.

"You got him?" Wesley said.

"I got him," Taylor replied. She stood up and dusted herself off as Simon writhed on the floor. She looked over her shoulder at Wesley— he was still standing, although a trickle of blood leaked through the sleeve of his shirt, where the black fabric had been torn. "You okay?"

"I'll live," Wesley replied. "Nice move."

"You're bleeding," Taylor said.

"Looks worse than it is."

Taylor almost laughed. Now he sounded like her whenever she got a wound on the job.

"Give me a hand," Taylor said, motioning to Simon. "We've got to get him to the car."

"Guys? I'm sorry I had to do this," Simon said. He looked scared and confused, like an animal who'd been captured.

"What were you doing?" Wesley asked.

"I was... I was protecting my garden," Simon replied.

"Your garden?" Taylor paused. "Why do you think we're here, Simon?"

"For my flowers. You're here to take them from me."

"No," Taylor said. "We're arresting you for the murder of Derek White."

"What? I didn't kill Derek White!"

"But you threatened to," Wesley said, holding his wound. Blood leaked out between his fingers. He was losing way more than Taylor had thought. They needed to get Wesley to a hospital. But first, they had to deal with Simon.

"I didn't kill anybody," Simon insisted. "That stuff, it was all just— it was all just a joke!"

"Do you think we're amused by your antics?" Taylor snapped.

"No—yes—no—I don't know. I don't know what I think," Simon said. "I know I didn't kill anybody. I didn't kill Derek White."

Taylor had enough of Simon's bullshit. Whether or not he was the Ghost Orchid Killer was yet to be determined—but he'd assaulted a federal agent, and that was more than enough to bring him in.

"Please," Simon said, "I'm sorry. I know I've been bad. But I didn't kill anyone!"

I'll be the judge of that, Taylor thought.

CHAPTER TWENTY

Taylor sat across from Simon in the interrogation room at Quantico, Wesley at her side with his wound bandaged up. Taylor and Wesley hadn't been working together long—but she felt confident in their ability to get this guy talking. So far, he'd only been blabbering nonsense, but this had to lead somewhere.

Taylor couldn't accept that it would be another dead end.

"Look," Simon said, "I know you think I'm a freak. But I didn't kill anyone. I swear."

Taylor resisted rolling her eyes. They'd been hearing a lot of that so far, and she was getting sick of it.

"Okay," Taylor said, "let's pretend for a moment that you're telling the truth, and that you didn't kill Derek White. Who did?"

"I don't know, I—"

"You were the one sending him threatening emails," Taylor said.

"What did you say again?" Wesley taunted. "That you were going to 'kill him?'"

"Okay," Simon said, "I sent the email, but really, me and the other guys—we invested in Derek's company, and he'd been stringing us along with lies for months. We just wanted to scare him a little. We didn't want him dead."

"Why not?" Taylor asked. "You sure liked sending him death *threats.*"

"Because he does have a family," Simon replied. "And me and the guys might be a little crazy—but we're not complete monsters. We would never have hurt anyone."

"Really?" Taylor asked. "Because as you can see, Agent Wesley here has a pretty bad mark."

"I'm sorry," Simon scrambled. "That was an accident. But we're just a bunch of middle-aged guys who never grew up. The threats were just jokes. We'd never hurt anyone on purpose."

"So, who killed Derek White?" Taylor asked.

"It wasn't me," Simon replied. "It wasn't any of the guys. You've gotta believe me."

Taylor studied the man in front of her. Simon was balding, and he had the face of a geek. He looked like the kind of guy who sat in his

99

house, making scary movies for the internet. On the surface, he seemed harmless enough; but Taylor couldn't forget the way he'd assaulted Wesley with those scissors, like it was nothing to him at all. He'd cracked upon being caught and cowered with his tail between his legs, but that made it all worse—it showed how unhinged he really was.

Simon Gibbons seemed like a good prospect.

There was only one issue.

Security footage from last night, at a local McDonald's, caught Simon's car as he went through the drive-thru. More security footage had shown him going home; they'd done a pass on his plates, and he hadn't been close to the crime scene. Or at least, his car hadn't.

Simon was the only lead they had, though. And if he was lying, then they were back to square one. Taylor and Wesley hadn't revealed the McDonald's detail yet.

"I don't believe you," Taylor said. "This is a murder investigation. You refuse to cooperate with us, you're going to jail."

Simon looked confused. "How would I know?"

"Because you're an orchid breeder," Wesley said. "We're looking for someone exactly like you, Simon. With the death threats in Derek's email, you're looking pretty guilty."

"What? No. I'm not an orchid breeder. I just—I grow flowers."

"Bullshit!" Wesley exclaimed, startling even Taylor. He was losing his patience. "You're an orchid breeder, and you killed Derek White. You're a killer, Simon. And we're going to prove it."

Wesley was clearly passionate about his work, but Taylor wanted to keep the energy in the room calm.

"Where have you been for the past three nights, Simon?" Taylor cut in. "Can anyone confirm your alibi?"

"I—I don't—" Simon stammered.

"Don't lie to us!" Wesley exclaimed.

"Y-yes," Simon said. "I've been attending lectures hosted by the Herb Garden. I was there last night! After that, I just went to McDonald's and then went home!"

"And the nights before?" Taylor asked.

"Well, I was home, but—"

"Can anyone confirm?" Taylor asked.

Simon averted his eyes. "No, no one can confirm."

Wesley's temper was flaring up again—Taylor could feel it coming, but she didn't want another outburst. It wasn't going anywhere. Even if Simon didn't have an alibi for the murders of Olivia and Zoe, if he did have one for the murder of Derek, then that would likely clear him. She was getting one of those gut feelings again. The ones that were almost always right. Something was telling her that Simon was yet another steppingstone to the real killer. He was not a criminal mastermind.

"We're wasting time," Taylor said. She stood up.

"Where are you going?" Wesley asked.

But she was already out of the room. Wesley chased after, and they reconvened outside the interrogation room. On the other side of the double-sided glass, Simon sulked in his chair.

"What are you thinking, Sage?" Wesley asked. "He's clearly our guy."

Taylor glanced through the double-sided glass. "I don't know. Something isn't right. What about the McDonald's footage?" She met Wesley's concerned, but attentive eyes. "I don't know if he's our guy."

"He could've left his car at home and gone out in another one, Sage," Wesley said.

"I don't know," Taylor said. "It's not adding up. Does he seem like a calculating killer to you?"

Wesley sighed. Taylor could tell that he was frustrated. She couldn't blame him—she was frustrated too. This case was getting to her, and she couldn't bear the idea of finding another victim with another damn ghost orchid. An innocent person deemed "fake" by some psychotic maniac. It wasn't right. It was their job to catch him.

"Look, Special Agent Sage," Wesley said, "I don't care if you have a hunch. He's a threat to society. I'm not done with him yet."

They held each other's hardened gazes, neither backing down. Taylor wouldn't budge—neither would Wesley. They were like two mountains facing off.

But Taylor didn't care. Wesley could do whatever Wesley wanted to do. He wasn't her boss, and Taylor had other plans.

"That's fine, Special Agent Wesley," Taylor said. "I'm going to look into this further. You go ahead and interrogate him. I'll be back."

Taylor went to walk away. Maybe it would be better to work alone, anyway, without Wesley's hotheadedness. But as she was reaching the door, Wesley's gritty voice stopped her.

"Hold on, Sage."

She faced him. A hesitant look was written on his rugged face, and he averted his eyes. Taylor crossed her arms and waited for an explanation.

"I know my teamwork needs work," Wesley said. "If you have a hunch, I should have your back."

Taylor considered what he was saying, and she relaxed her tense shoulders. "I don't expect you to do everything I say, Wes. If you want to stay here, that's fine, but I'm going."

"We're supposed to do this together, right?" he said. "What do you think we should do next?"

It was a simple question, but it meant a lot. It meant he was willing to work with her, and Taylor appreciated that.

"We should rip up his alibi," Taylor said. "We should find out everything we can about the guys in the email, and about Simon. We should do everything we can to get to the bottom of this. I think we should run down that alibi hosted by the Herb Garden he mentioned."

Wesley didn't look too pleased, but he nodded. "Let's check it out."

CHAPTER TWENTY ONE

Taylor walked into the lecture hall in Pine Point with Wesley. There were various posters set up, advertising the Herb Garden in D.C., which was hosting the event here. It was a massive lecture hall that reminded Taylor more of an amphitheater. Rows upon rows of seating were stacked high. The theater was only about half full, though—mostly filled with young students.

At the bottom, a man in a corduroy suit spoke into a microphone, reading off a paper. On the white board was a drawing of an herb. *Professor Van der Werff* was written on the other side of the board. Taylor and Wesley sat at the very top, gaining a few looks from attendees, who quickly went back to watching the professor's lecture.

Professor Van der Werff adjusted his glasses, looking at the paper he was holding. His withered, yet somehow loud voice filled the hall. "Fennel is a highly underrated herb, I'd say. A milder flavor than its more popular cousins, anise and coriander. It is also one of the best sources of fiber you can get. And it helps reduce gas, as well as being used in herbal medicine as a decongestant. It can also be used to treat indigestion, tumors and as a treatment for kidney disease. Fennel is also good for diabetics, as it lowers blood glucose levels."

Taylor listened intently, although this talk of food reminded her of Ben. Her heart hurt again, remembering their phone call last night. She stifled it down. Not the time.

The professor continued on, talking about medicinal herbs. "The focus of this lecture is not on culinary herbs. We will be talking about culinary herbs and spices later this week, in a weeklong lecture. Today, we will be focusing on herbal medicine and how herbs can heal with a few side dishes to the main lecture. With that said, are there any questions?"

His words were met with silence and polite applause.

An hour passed, and the lecture was almost done. A few questions from the audience, and then it was over. The crowd began to file out, and Wesley and Taylor waited for a few moments for the professor, who was taking questions from the audience.

"Thank you all for joining me and thank you for your questions. My next lecture will be in two weeks, on the properties of black pepper."

103

Taylor and Wesley made their way to the professor.

Professor Van der Werff adjusted his glasses again, then his eyes widened when Taylor and Wesley showed their badges.

"Oh, hello," the professor said. "How may I help you?"

"Hi there," Taylor said. "I'm Special Agent Taylor Sage, and this is my partner, Special Agent Wesley. We were wondering if you could confirm if someone was in attendance here last night." Taylor pulled out her phone with a picture of Simon's mugshot. "Do you recognize this man?"

"Oh, yes!" the professor exclaimed. "That's Simon. He's extremely enthusiastic about plants. He was here late last night."

"What time did he leave?"

"Hmm, I think it was around 3:20 a.m."

Taylor felt a pit in her stomach. That lined up with Simon's story. The security footage had caught him at the McDonald's at four a.m. So if he could be accounted before then, then that meant that Taylor's hunch was right. Simon Gibbons wasn't their guy.

"Thank you so much," Taylor said. "If you could send us your contact information, we may like to interview you further."

The professor wrote on a business card and handed it to Taylor.

"My address is on there," the professor said. "I'm in the middle of moving, so I can be reached by email for the next couple of weeks."

"Thanks," Wesley muttered.

Taylor thanked him again, and she and Wesley left the lecture hall. Outside, the sun was setting, and a cool breeze wafted over Taylor's skin, giving her goosebumps. She and Wesley faced each other under the lights of the lecture hall.

"Guess your hunch was right," Wesley said. "Good call, Sage."

"Thanks," Taylor mumbled, feeling awkward being complimented by Wesley. Still, frustration coursed through her—they'd wasted so much time here, and it had led them to nothing but a dead end.

"Guess we should break for the night," Wesley said. "We're at a dead end. Least we know who the killer isn't."

"I could still go for a few hours, try to figure something out," Taylor said. She remembered how, earlier, Wesley had kept working over their "lunch" break. She supposed now was as good of a time as any to bring it up. "Wes, by the way," she said as they began walking to the parking lot. "Earlier, at lunch. I would've stayed and worked with you."

"Guess I didn't think about it," he muttered. "You said you wanted lunch."

104

"If you knew me, you'd know I'm always the one who skips meals to keep working." She paused. "I did meet up with my father, though, to help build more of a profile on the killer."

He glanced at her and lifted an eyebrow. "Oh?"

"He's a clinical psychologist. My dad, I mean."

"Interesting. What did he say?"

"He mostly built upon what we already had. We're looking for a bitter, angry, resentful man, likely with a history of trauma and abuse in his background."

"I'd agree with him there."

They reached the car. Wesley went to the driver side and spoke to her over the roof of the sedan.

"I'm still thinking we should break for the night," he said. "I need to get home. That okay?"

"Of course," Taylor said. "We can start fresh in the morning."

They got into the car, Taylor in the passenger seat, Wesley behind the wheel. Silence took over them. Wesley had said he needed to go home, but it occurred to Taylor that she didn't know anything about her new partner on a personal level. In fact, she didn't even know his full name.

"Wesley..." Taylor started. "Can I ask you something personal?"

"Yeah," Wesley said, the car in idle. "I guess."

"What's your full name? It can't just be Wesley."

Wesley looked at her, his expression apathetic. "Wesley's the only name you need to know."

Taylor gave him a *look*. "Don't be all cryptic. I'm your partner. I can find out your name. I just haven't looked into it. Teamwork, remember?" Even Taylor herself wasn't this mysterious with her partners. She'd sort of let Calvin in before. Sort of.

To her surprise, Wesley half-smiled. Maybe he did have a sense of humor hidden somewhere in there.

"It's John Wesley," he said. "But John is my father's name. I don't like it. So just call me Wesley."

"Oh," was all she could think to say.

When Taylor said nothing else, Wesley started driving. Taylor sank in the passenger seat. She found herself curious about him, and this was the first real "open" thing he'd told her about himself. Taylor wanted to know more—and it was in her nature to ask questions.

"So, uh, do you have any kids?"

"One. A daughter. Why?"

"Just making conversation," Taylor said. "It can be hard, getting to know people. Sometimes you just have to ask."

"True enough," Wesley said. He focused on the road, then: "Any other prying questions you've been wondering about me?"

Taylor nearly rolled her eyes. "I'm not trying to be nosy, Wesley."

"Relax, I'm messing with you. We can talk about ourselves if you want. Or we can just sit here in silence till we get back to HQ."

"You have any family?" Taylor quickly seized the opportunity to know more.

"No wife or girlfriend," he said. "My family is my daughter and my daughter alone."

It struck a personal chord for Taylor. She'd always had the husband, but no kid. And now she'd never have a kid of her own. Unless what Belasco "predicted" was true, but Taylor knew better than to get her hopes up too high.

"What about your daughter's mom?" Taylor asked. "Is she involved?"

"She's fine. We raise Maisie together. She looks after her when I'm working." Wesley glanced at Taylor as he drove. "I guess we haven't really exchanged any life stories, Special Agent Sage. Maybe we should, though, to make sure there are no surprises."

Surprises? It almost sounded like a warning, like he had some sort of dark secret to share. Taylor's curiosity piqued. "What do you mean?"

"Like, say there was an incident in my past, and my new partner found out about it by chance and felt like she'd been lied to. I'm sure you'd ask me to step down."

"I wouldn't do that," Taylor said. She certainly had her own laundry list of "incidents" from her past, ones she'd rather not discuss. But Wesley had captured her attention, and she needed to know now. "We all have skeletons. What incident in your past?"

Wesley kept his eyes on the road, but Taylor could tell he was thinking about something. "When I was in my twenties, I fucked up an undercover mission. As you know, I can be a bit hotheaded. I put my cover at risk. One of the criminals had a relative who was a little kid. I let my guard down, and we got caught.

"The thing is, I got into a situation that I couldn't get out of, and I ended up shooting two undercover officers to save my cover. One was in the shoulder, but the other was in the thigh. I didn't wanna kill the guys, obviously. But I didn't realize it at the time—in fact, nobody realized it—but the guy whose leg I shot. He ended up being paralyzed."

That sounded bad. Really bad. "What happened to him?"

Wesley's hands tensed on the wheel; his eyes narrowed. "He was young, inexperienced. But he still can't move that leg, as far as I know. He had to quit being a cop. It just didn't work for him anymore." He paused. "There were no charges for the incident because I was an undercover agent. But I was ashamed about what I did. I went off the grid, became an auto-mechanic, and had a kid with my ex-girlfriend. I didn't want anyone to know what had happened. No one did. I hid. But then a couple years later, I realized I was hiding from the world and from myself. So I decided to come back to work. I'm a much better person for it."

More silence fell over them as Taylor took in Wesley's story.

"I'm mostly back for her," he said. "For Maisie, my daughter. FBI agents get paid a hell of a lot more than mechanics. I want her to have a good future."

"Then I'm glad you're here," Taylor said. "You're doing a good job. I'm sure you're a hero to your daughter."

Wesley didn't say anything, still tense and quiet.

"I'm no hero," he eventually said. "I don't want to be a legend for helping people. I want to make sure my daughter never has to worry about paying for college. Never has to worry about getting a career or a house. I want to make sure she has the life her mother and I could never have."

By the end of his speech, Taylor's heart hurt. She didn't know what to say to Wesley, but she admired him for his candor.

"Thanks for telling me all that, Wes," Taylor said. "It means a lot to know who my partner really is."

"You'd find out eventually," he said. His gray eyes flicked to hers, then back on the road. "But nothing in life is free, Sage. Tell me about you. Kids? Husband?"

Taylor laughed and shook her head. She wouldn't even know where to begin talking about herself.

But she realized then that she'd kept so much inside—the only one who even knew about her marital issues was Belasco.

"My husband left me not long ago," Taylor confessed. "I didn't tell Winchester. Or even my parents."

"Damn. Sorry," Wesley said.

"It's because I can't have kids."

Wesley's eyes found hers. Taylor looked away, but she didn't feel vulnerable. She was just being honest. Like he'd done for her. Taylor didn't know how much of a weight it would be off her to just tell someone that. To tell someone the truth.

"When I was in my twenties, I was reckless," Taylor said. "More reckless than I am now. I threw myself into a dangerous situation, and I got shot. The bullet pierced my abdomen, and, well, I guess it did damage to other parts too. I recently found out that I can't have kids because of something that happened nearly a decade ago."

"And your husband left you, just like that?" Wesley lifted a brow.

"More or less," Taylor said. "He could still come back. I don't know."

"Would you want him to?"

"At this point, I'm not sure," she admitted. She thought of their conversation yesterday, and it was like a punch to the gut all over again. She'd been suppressing it, but now that they were out of work, Taylor knew she'd have to face it again.

"I won't tell the boss you're having troubles at home," Wesley said. "That's between us."

Taylor smiled. "Thanks, Wesley. I trust you."

They'd only been working together a short time, but she meant that.

CHAPTER TWENTY TWO

Taylor's hands gripped the steering wheel of her car as she drove into Pelican Beach, darkness taking over the sky. She didn't want to go home. She didn't want to sleep, cold and alone in that house. She knew she'd have to eventually but found herself driving toward downtown. Pelican Beach had an exciting nightlife in the summertime, during tourist season, but now that school was back in, things had calmed down.

Two things had plagued her on the ride up—the first being the case. Taylor knew it was only a matter of time before the next victim lost their life, but she felt like she was hitting her head over and over again at every turn. They were getting closer, yet nowhere at all. She sighed.

The second thing was, of course, Ben, and that phone call yesterday. Had that really been another woman in the background?

Could he move on so soon?

It was too painful to think about, so Taylor drove down the strip, past all the restaurants, bars, and shops, moving farther and farther from home, not really sure where she was going. She could stop by the bookstore and pick up something to read. Or maybe she'd stop at the drugstore and pick up toothpaste. They—she—was running low.

She attended to the street as she drove, even as she found it increasingly harder to focus on what was in front of her.

She geared her mind back to the case. Yes, everything with Ben had been one of the worst experiences of her life. But her job was bigger than that. It was about saving lives.

And there was one person in Pelican Beach who had helped Taylor do that before.

She pulled her car outside of Belasco's shop.

It was far past closing time, and yet a light was on inside. Taylor wondered if Belasco lived here as well—it looked like there was an apartment above the shop. She knocked on the door and heard shuffling inside. The door opened, and Taylor was once again assaulted with the plume of energy that accompanied the psychic.

"Mrs. Sage, you can't be here," she said, looking down on Taylor. "I'm closed."

"I know," Taylor said. "I... I'd really love to talk. About my case.

And who I think could be next. I wouldn't come if it wasn't important."

Belasco paused, and a small smile formed on her lips. "All right. Come in."

Belasco turned and walked into the shop. Taylor followed; she had never been in the shop past closing, and Belasco had long let the sticks of intense burn out. The smell still lingered in the air as Taylor followed Belasco though the curtain, to the dark back of the shop. Belasco turned on the light and filled the room with a soft yellow glow.

The tarot cards waited on the table, as always, ready for her.

Taylor swallowed the knot in her throat as she sat down on one end, Belasco on the other.

"I was just cleaning up the shop," Belasco said. "You caught me before I went upstairs for dinner. But I knew you'd be back." She smiled solemnly. "I don't think I could pay to keep you away, at this point, Mrs. Sage."

"I don't want to take up too much of your time," Taylor said, feeling guilty. At this point, coming here was almost like an addiction.

"Yes. So, let's get started. You said you're worried about a case. Let's get you a reading and see if we can learn anything." Belasco flipped up the first tarot card. "The Lovers," she said. "Interesting. These cards speak of change. The Lovers indicates that there is someone very important to you or will be soon. It could be a new lover, or a close friend. Someone whose presence will change your life."

Taylor's stomach churned. She resisted the urge to check her phone, to see if maybe Ben had called.

"But there is also a negative side," Belasco said. "The Lovers card indicates that something will block your path. This is why I pulled it— it doesn't mean that there is someone out there. It means that there is something within yourself. You are your own worst enemy. There is a great force in your own dark heart, trying to destroy you from within. It's extremely powerful, and it's working on your subconscious. You must be careful. You must trust your instincts, Mrs. Sage."

Taylor thought back to earlier this morning, when she'd lost herself thinking about Angie. Was this what Belasco was referring to?

Belasco flipped up the second card.

"The Tower," she said. "This card represents a breakdown of your current system. A great earthquake—it could be mental, emotional, or even physical. An unexpected great collapse. You need to be ready for this. This is your call to action. You must move fast."

Taylor's eyes widened as she looked at the card, then back at Belasco.

"There's a killer out there," she whispered. "And he's about to strike again. Where?"

"I'm not sure," Belasco said. "Whether he's going to attack someone you know, or someone in particular, I don't know. I only see a body of water. I only see danger."

"So what do I do?"

"I can't answer that, Mrs. Sage," Belasco said. "Now, for the final card..." She flipped up the third card.

Taylor's heart skipped.

"The Devil," Belasco said. "One of the major arcana cards in the tarot deck, representing all things evil. This card indicates that the only way to avoid the destruction in the Tower card is to go down a path you do not want. This is a path of darkness. You must go to the Devil if you want to find your way out of The Tower."

Taylor just stared at the Devil card.

"What do they mean?" she asked.

"It's... hard to say," Belasco said. "This is a rather convoluted reading, if I'm being honest." She paused. "If I had to interpret these in one way... I would say it means you aren't looking deep enough within yourself for the answers. You know what you need to do, somewhere inside you, but you're repressing it." Belasco peered at her beneath her long lashes. "Perhaps your trouble at home is bleeding into work without you realizing it."

"No," Taylor said. At least, she didn't think so. She always brought her A game to work. It was second nature to her.

But maybe there was something she was missing.

Those cards were still on the table, mocking her. She had no answers. She saw only darkness.

Realizing she'd overstayed her welcome, Taylor stood up. "Thank you so much," she said. "I... I'm sorry if this was inconvenient. I'll make sure to read up on the Devil card if I can."

Belasco nodded. "Goodnight, Mrs. Sage."

Taylor said a quick goodbye, dashing out of the shop.

She knew she was missing something. Something big.

But for now, she needed to get home, so she got into her car and began the drive. As she drove through the streets of Pelican Beach, she thought about what Belasco had said.

This killer was going to strike again. And he would bring down destruction.

And Taylor was determined to end it. But she was missing something; she knew it.

At this hour, the streets of Pelican Beach were empty, as if the townspeople had all already made their way to bed. The streetlights glowed orange, and their light spilled down onto the streets.

She turned onto her street, finding her quiet and dark house. She pulled into the driveway and sighed, thinking about what Belasco said. The answer was within her...

She closed her eyes. What was her gut telling her to do?

She felt so tired. And the answer was right there, somewhere within her. She just couldn't see it.

Maybe it was time to turn off her brain and just act on instinct.

And her instincts were telling her to take out her phone and do some research. As if on autopilot, she took out her phone and began searching the victims. She wasn't sure what she was looking for, but she kept clicking through articles. There were many on Zoe Duntz, especially, and about her death. Taylor tried adjusting the time frame to before the first murder, but nothing, at a glance, came up that could link all three of them.

But another idea occurred to her—one she hadn't tried yet.

Using quotation marks, she searched the exact name of each victim: "Olivia Newman." "Zoe Duntz." "Derek White." To see if their names had ever all been in the same spot before they were killed.

One result came up.

A local news website in Pine Point.

CHAPTER TWENTY THREE

The driver crept up alongside her as she walked through the early morning. Disgusting. Filthy. A true fake. He hated the way she carried herself, as if she were a true intellectual. But he knew the truth. She was on her way to tell more lies, and he couldn't let her.

He pulled his car up beside her on the street. Since it was six a.m., there was no one around. She was looking at her phone, oblivious to the world, when he let down his window.

"Excuse me?" he called out.

She looked at him with a tolerant expression, trying to place his face. "Good morning. Can I help you?"

Gross, mousy voice. He hated her. Hated everything she stood for.

He smiled, looking into her eyes. He had practiced this look, knew how to make it glow with warmth. "I couldn't help but notice you're out here walking all alone. My last client just canceled on me. Interested in a ride?"

She looked around cautiously. "Um... no thank you."

"I don't mind, really." He rolled his car up alongside her. "I'll take you wherever you want to go. No strings attached."

"No, thank you." Her voice was firm.

He nodded, turning his wheel to pull away. She would be a tough one to crack. "Suit yourself, then," he said. "Have a nice day."

He pulled into a parking lot and waited. She walked away, not looking back.

Anger fumed inside of him as he sat alone. How dare she reject him? How dare she reject all of them? He swallowed his anger, letting it simmer deep within him. He'd have to find a way to make her change her mind. But this rejection was not an option.

"Fuck you, you stupid bitch!" he screamed. His voice echoed out into the empty morning. "I'll show you... show you all..."

He looked into the rear-view mirror, studying his reflection. Staring, he thought how much he could change. He could become a better man. He could get a better car and a better job. He could become a better person.

He wouldn't be a fake. Not like them.

He deserved what they had.

They were not better than him.

That bitch deserved to be punished.

They were all fakes.

His phone rang, cutting through the silence. He picked it up, muting the ring. It was his mother. She'd been trying to reach him all morning.

She was the fakest of them all. He didn't want to talk to her. He didn't want to talk to anyone.

Sitting alone in the quiet, his memories of the past came flooding back to him. He had never been a fake. Never been a whore. How could they treat him like this?

He worked his fingers over his phone, feeling the smooth, sleek surface. He chewed the inside of his cheek, thinking. His lips curled into a snarl.

He turned the key in the ignition, listening as it sputtered to life. He pulled out onto the street and drove away. He pressed down on the gas, sending his car speeding down the road. He had to find a way to get the girl in his car. If not today, then soon.

She would pay—all in good time.

For now, he had no choice but to give up and move on. He couldn't risk getting caught; it would be the end of his plans. Foolish police officers. They were like chickens with their heads cut off, trying to figure out who was leaving the bodies. It was him—it was all him.

He began his drive back home, through the early morning, through the livening town.

He drove on and on, past the gaunt, hunched-over people. They were all so empty. So fake.

They were all the same.

She was the same as they were.

He didn't need them.

They were all fakes.

They were all whores.

He swallowed his anger and rage, keeping his emotions deep inside of him. He wasn't going to let this get to him. He was in control. He was smarter than they were, and he was going to prove it.

They would learn their place.

When he got home, he went straight for the backyard. Mother's orchids grew in the garden, and he clipped one off on his way to his art studio. Mother told everyone they were hers, but it was the gardener who kept them alive. Stupid, fake Mother.

He entered his studio and locked the door. Finally free. In his safe haven.

Delicately, he placed the orchid on his work table and got out his white paints. He stared lovingly at the flower.

I will make you beautiful, he thought. *Beautiful, but fake.*

CHAPTER TWENTY FOUR

Taylor scrolled through articles on her laptop in the briefing room at Quantico, Wesley across from her doing the same. Pine Point Daily had featured the victims, Olivia Newman, Zoe Duntz, and Derek White in articles, all within the last two months. As soon as Taylor had figured that out, she'd zipped back to Quantico and called Wesley to get him in too.

Now, Taylor and Wesley were scrolling through more articles to see if they could spot who the next victim might be. This was the connection—this was how the killer was selecting his targets. It had to be. But so far, Taylor hadn't found anyone who seemed overly "fake," who might gain a spot on the killer's hitlist.

"Any luck?" Taylor asked Wesley.

It was late—after ten p.m.—but both of them had come back to HQ with coffees, ready to pull an all-nighter if necessary. Wesley looked tired and grumpy, though. He just shook his head and went back to reading his own screen.

"I found a story on this guy, Nate Martin, who works for Pine Point Resort," Taylor said, taking a few seconds to explain. "I thought he might be a victim. Maybe the next one. But he's not the type. He's a big guy—works out—and he likes to ski. Loved by all, apparently, and very genuine."

"So he's not our guy," Wesley said.

"I guess not."

Taylor sighed, flipped her sleek black hair behind her ears, then stretched her neck out and down to the left, popping the vertebrae. She was exhausted, and her eyes felt heavy. But she couldn't stop now. They were hunting for an article that featured someone who could be construed as a "fake," someone who the killer might choose to kill next. But Taylor had been looking into the names of most of the people featured, and they all came up clean.

She kept hearing that little voice in the back of her head. The one that told her to think about the case. About the victims. About looking within herself for the answers. She closed her eyes and tapped her finger on the table in a random beat, trying to clear her mind. She was too tired to think about it anymore. Nothing was coming to her.

With a sigh, Taylor continued combing through articles. One of these had to lead somewhere.

She stopped on an article about a school principal named Sherry Yates. The article was about how helpful Sherry had been to the Pine Point high school community. She didn't immediately flag as a potential victim.

But when Taylor looked Sherry up on a separate browser, she found a different story.

A headline read:

PINE POINT HIGH SCHOOL PRINCIPAL ACCUSED OF ALTERING STUDENT TEST SCORES.

Taylor's breath caught in her throat. This could be who they were looking for.

"Wes, look at this," Taylor said.

Sluggishly, he came over to her laptop and peered at the screen. "Who's Sherry Yates?" Wesley asked.

"Principal of Pine Point High School," Taylor said. "I think this might be our next victim."

"But she's not a fake, is she? I mean, she's a school administrator."

"That's not what she was accused of," Taylor said. "She was accused of faking her students' test scores to make them seem better. She could be construed as a fake."

Wesley nodded. "She could be our next victim."

"Exactly." Taylor stood up abruptly. "Wes, we need to talk to Sherry Yates and get her in protective custody."

Wesley threw his jacket over his shoulder. "Let's go."

***

Taylor knocked on the door to Sherry's small, two-story house. It was the only one on the block with the lights off and an SUV in the driveway. There were no cars out on the street, either. Probably because it was cold and dark. As the wind picked up, Taylor shivered.

After making some phone calls, Taylor and Wesley had driven down to Sherry Yates's house in Pine Point with a couple of uniformed officers joining them. The other two were waiting in their cruisers on the street. It was late—Sherry may have been in bed. Or worse. Taylor prayed it wasn't the latter.

A few moments later, a middle-aged woman with long, salt-and-pepper hair answered the door. She was wearing a sweater and sweatpants.

"Mrs. Yates?" Taylor asked.

The woman blinked. "Yes?"

Taylor pulled out her badge. "I'm Special Agent Taylor Sage, FBI. This is Special Agent Wesley. We need to talk to you."

"What's this about?"

Taylor paused. "May we come in?"

She stood aside to let them come in. The home smelled of candles and had a calm ambience. Sherry turned on the dim lightning, so it wouldn't blind anyone.

"Is anyone home with you?" Taylor asked, looking around. Photos of Sherry and a man hung on the walls.

"No, my husband is out of town," Sherry said. "Here, come sit in the living room."

Taylor and Wesley followed Sherry to a comfortable room that was designed for relaxing. Soft furniture, candles, a throw rug over dark hardwood floors. A large picture window looked out over the pine trees.

"Would you like anything to drink?" Sherry offered. "Hot chocolate? Water?"

"No, thank you," Taylor said, sitting down on a plush, yellow couch. Wesley sat down beside her.

"I'm going to be honest with you, ma'am," Taylor said. "We believe your life is in danger. We've discovered recent events in the Pine Point area that lead us to believe that you may be the next victim."

Sherry went pale. "What?"

"The serial killer who's been terrorizing Pine Point has been targeting people who represent a fake. It's how he selects his victims."

Sherry looked like she was about to faint. "But I'm not a fake. I'm a principal."

"I know that," Taylor said. "But the killer might think you are. How did you feel when you were accused of 'fixing' your students' exams?"

"I, well—" Sherry paused. "I know it was wrong of me. But if my students didn't get an above average score, the board was going to cut our funding. We'd lose most of the computers in the computer lab. And the library... we'd lose so much."

Taylor nodded. She had read that online, as well. Most people seemed to defend Sherry's decision. It could be construed as "fake," yes, but it was also altruistic. A seed of doubt was planted within Taylor.

What if Sherry *wasn't* the next victim?

Sherry put her hands over her mouth. "Oh my God, this can't be happening…"

"We need to get you into protective custody for the night, at least," Wesley said. "It's for your safety."

Sherry took her hands away from her mouth and shook her head. "I can't leave my house."

Taylor and Wesley exchanged a look. "It's not a choice you have," Taylor said. "Wesley, can you escort her out?"

Wesley nodded. "Please follow me, Mrs. Yates."

Although apprehensive, Sherry followed Wesley outside, leaving Taylor alone in the quiet house. One of the officers stationed outside was ready to bring Sherry to a safe house. The other would stick around to help stake the house out with Taylor and Wesley, to see if the killer made an appearance.

Taylor stood up and made her way around the house. It was a small, but well-kept place. There were no photos of the kids or classrooms. There was one picture of Sherry, her husband, and her parents, though. It must have been from her wedding.

Taylor began ruminating over the case. The other victims had been self-serving. But Sherry—she did what she'd done for the greater good. Taylor began to doubt, more and more, that Sherry was the true target.

Which meant that she had to look at the other victims again.

Just then, Wesley came back in. "Okay, she's safe. We should still stake out here, see if the guy shows up. Just in case."

Taylor chewed on her lip, hesitating to tell Wesley what was really on her mind. He stepped up to her, sensing it.

"What's going on?" he asked.

"I'm... just not so sure if Sherry is the right target."

Wesley raised an eyebrow. "You serious?"

She paused, wondering how to phrase what she was feeling. "It's just... the targets haven't only been 'fakes.' They were also self-serving. Sherry didn't do what she did for herself, she did it for her students."

Wesley was quiet, and Taylor anticipated his response. He eventually said, "I respect your knowledge, Sage, but we don't have enough of a profile on this guy to make calls like that."

"Maybe you're right," Taylor said. "But I think we should look at the articles again, see if there's anyone else in there."

"You're right. We'll get started on that first thing in the morning. Why don't you go home and get some rest? Or look more into it if you want, it's your call."

Taylor hesitated. "I can stay—"

"Go home," Wesley said. "I've got an officer outside. We can stake out here without you. I still think Sherry Yates is our most likely target."

Taylor hesitated. She didn't want it to seem like she was unhinged or walking away from the case for being "too tired." She wasn't. She was buzzing—she could do this all night.

But Taylor gave Wesley a quiet nod.

She would leave this up to him. But she had no intention of stopping her work.

CHAPTER TWENTY FIVE

Taylor went right back to Quantico, right back to her laptop to scour through articles on potential "fakes" who could be targets. There had to be someone else. Someone she'd missed before. But as she hunted through names, looking each of them up, she came up empty-handed.

Frustrated, Taylor pressed her palms into her eyes and sighed. It was late now—or rather, early, pushing 4:30 a.m. Time had flown by, and she was exhausted. But this case was too close for her to stop now.

Pine Point Daily posted dozens of articles a week. They were extremely popular with the student population in town, mostly covering articles on local businesses and entrepreneurs. That's what Derek, Olivia, and Zoe's articles had been centered on. Their rise to success.

As Taylor scanned through another article, she took note of the editor's name at the top. John Penn. Interesting—she had been so focused on looking for victims before, that she hadn't stopped to check out who was actually writing these articles.

She clicked on another article. Also by John Penn.

Her fingers flew over the keyboard as she checked every article that had been posted since the first victim had been found.

In almost every single one, John Penn was the author or editor.

Taylor's heart rate picked up. She started searching the web. John was the editor-in-chief at Pine Point Daily and wrote every article the victims had been featured in. He had also written a million different articles that featured other people. Clearly, this John guy knew the paper inside and out.

She did some quick recon on him—just in case—to see if he fit the profile they'd been building of the killer. John was forty-seven, had no priors, and came from an average background, with two parents who worked in the publishing industry. He had a wife, two kids, and seemed to be living an overall happy life.

He'd also been writing for the Pine Point for over two decades. So for him to start randomly murdering "fakes" now, when his work seemed to do nothing but praise them, seemed unlikely.

No... Taylor didn't get the sense John Penn was the killer. But a thought occurred to her: she could spend her whole life combing through these articles—but maybe John could help streamline the process.

***

Forty minutes later, Taylor sat in an all-night breakfast diner in Pine Point, her hands clasped over a cup of coffee. She was jittery and trying not to think of much else as she waited for John Penn to show up. She'd been lucky that he was awake and had promptly responded to her email inquiry. Writers never sleep, apparently.

"Special Agent Sage?" a voice asked.

Taylor lifted her head. A short man with glasses stood above her. She recognized him from the website—this was John Penn.

"John," Taylor said. "Thank you so much for meeting with me."

"My pleasure." He sat across from her. He was a jittery guy, dressed in a T-shirt and jeans. He had thick, curly hair and a beard. He looked like he'd be more comfortable being a barista than the editor-in-chief of the Pine Point Daily. "So, how can I help out?"

"I was hoping you could help me with an investigation I'm conducting," Taylor said. "It's about the serial killer in Pine Point."

Penn frowned. "Oh, it's been all over the news. One of my teams that covers more serious stories has been all over it."

"Right. And you are the editor of the Pine Point Daily. How did you start writing?"

"I've always loved writers. Hemingway, Steinbeck, Fitzgerald, those kinds of guys. I used to dream of escaping my small town and becoming a writer myself. But instead, I became a high school English teacher. And I was okay with that, but I still wanted to write, so I started a blog. I was posting articles on my blog, and then the Pine Point Daily approached me and asked if I could write for them, too. So I did."

"So, you've written a lot for the paper?" Taylor asked.

"I have."

"Good." She paused. It was time to get to the point; John seemed trustworthy, at least at face value. "I've been looking for someone, and I think you might be able to help me."

"What do you need?" he said, leaning forward.

"I'm looking for someone who may have been featured in your paper who could be construed as a 'fake.'"

Penn lifted an eyebrow. "That's rather broad. Can you be more specific?"

Taylor nodded. "As I'm sure you know, three people have been killed in Pine Point recently. All three of them were featured in articles in Pine Point Daily: Olivia Newman, Zoe Duntz, and Derek White."

Penn's face went pale. "I remember those articles. I admit, I was shocked to hear all three of them had died... but... I didn't think anything about the fact that I'd featured them in the paper. I mean, their articles were all pretty far apart."

He continued to stare at her. Taylor stared back.

"So you didn't think it was weird that you'd written about all three of them?" she asked.

"I mean, yes, it did seem weird. I figured it was just a coincidence. I've been at the paper for a really long time—people started coming to me for advice, for career advice, and I wrote about them for publicity."

"Did any of the three victims request to be written about?"

"Olivia and Zoe did. Derek, we approached ourselves, but he practically begged us to do the feature once we were already there. We usually charge people to feature them, but we didn't charge these three because we found them so interesting. Plus, they were locals."

Taylor frowned. "But wouldn't it make more sense for you to write about the people who actually bought the ad space?"

"I know what you're saying, but I have to pay for the paper somehow. So I advertise a lot. In fact, out of every article we post, at least half of them are advertisements. Not just big ones, but small ones, too. Anything from a coupon for ten dollars off your purchase at a men's clothing store to a small bodega in the area advertising the newest type of granola bar. But paid content isn't always interesting. We wanted to feature people like Olivia, Zoe, and Derek, so we put them in free of charge. In fact, Zoe drove our views up. Does that help?"

Taylor considered this. She wasn't sure it did.

"Right," Taylor said. "The thing is that the connection between these three victims is that they've all been caught in 'self-serving' lies. Olivia, with her plastic surgery. Zoe, Photoshopping herself on social media. And Derek, lying to the shareholders in his company."

"I see," Penn said. "So you're looking for another person in that vein? To what, try to determine the next victim?"

"Exactly," Taylor said. "But not just somebody who lied. Somebody who is doing it for their own self gain."

Penn leaned back in the booth and stroked his beard. "There is actually one name that comes to mind."

Taylor perked up. "Who?"

"Someone at our paper, actually. Julia Rose. She's young, fresh out of college, and new. She made a mistake recently and we had to pull her article. Her sources were insufficient, and 'misinformation' isn't a word PPD wants associated with it."

Taylor's pulse jumped into her throat. Julia Rose. This could be the next target.

"Where can I find her?"

"She always comes into work extremely early," Penn said, checking his watch. "She normally walks in and is there by six a.m. sharp. She's a good kid, just inexperienced."

"And you're sure she's on the up-and-up?" Taylor said.

"Yes," Penn said. "She's normally a very sweet person. But she's also very ambitious. With only a few months in the business, she's already trying to prove herself. Which is a dangerous game, in my opinion."

Taylor leaned back, taking it all in. This Julia Rose could be their next target. And if that was the case, she needed to act fast. "Could you do me a favor and send her address to my phone?" she asked Penn.

"Sure thing." He pulled out his phone and tapped away.

Taylor stood up. "Thanks for your help, John. This has been invaluable."

"I hope so," he said. "It's good to help the FBI. Do you think this is going to help you catch the killer?"

"I'm going to do everything in my power to make sure it does."

She knew in her heart that this was the right path. That she was going to finally catch the serial killer, who'd haunted Pine Point for the past week. It was now or never.

Taylor checked her watch. 5:34 a.m. She was already in Pine Point.

If she hurried now, she could catch Julia at home—before the killer got her.

CHAPTER TWENTY SIX

This was it. His big moment. He wouldn't let her go this time.

As the driver crept up to the girl's house, she hadn't taken notice of him. Not yet. But she would, soon enough. He could see her through the window, getting ready for a "hard" day at work. Hard, meaning sitting around on her ass and making up lies. Faking things to all the other fakers.

His ribbon was draped lovingly in the passenger seat. This time, he didn't care if she agreed to come in—no, he would come to her. It was a bit of a game plan change for him, as he liked his art to be displayed in public, but that was okay. He could move her later.

She didn't stand a chance.

Finally, more justice. The itch was too strong to resist scratching. He had to make this faker pay. He hated her—he hated everything she stood for.

He hated everything in the world.

Even himself.

Memories from long ago slithered into his mind. Mother. She was so phony, with her big fake hair, fake lips, fake breasts.

Father. He was such a scheming liar. He cheated on everything he ever did. He didn't deserve even an ounce of the wealth he had.

Fakers. All of them.

But the driver; he could never kill them. He couldn't... he needed them alive. At least, for now he did.

So instead, he would send them a message.

They would see it on their TVs. The beautiful, fake ghost orchids; the beautiful, dead people.

He had so much planned.

He couldn't wait to see their faces.

But first, he had to take care of this girl. He had to take care of these flowers.

He glanced back at the ribbon—the beautiful, red ribbon—and smiled. His finely crafted ghost orchid, as fake as his next target, was in a glass box next to the ribbon. In perfect condition.

"Today's the day," he said. "I'm going to make it happen."

He took the fake flower, picked up his ribbon, and got out of his car.

They won't be able to ignore this.

He walked up the slight incline to her little house, passing the neighbors' cars.

They didn't even bother to take down their Christmas lights. Some of their cars were overflowing with trash.

He didn't like the world he was in.

He liked the world he was going to create.

He would smile when he was the ruler. And everyone would smile with him.

Or they would die.

The lights on her porch were on, so he walked up to the door and slid his key into the lock. The key he'd stolen from her work and replicated. He walked into her living room, plopping the fake flower on the coffee table, and sat down on the couch.

He would stay here, waiting for her.

She would wake up soon. Go for her morning Cheerios.

And then, he would strike.

CHAPTER TWENTY SEVEN

Taylor sped toward Julia Rose's house as the crack of dawn began to paint the sky. If Taylor was lucky, Julia wouldn't have left for work yet—Taylor could still catch her. She could still save her life.

As she drove, she called Wesley. He was still staking out Sherry's house, as far as Taylor knew. He promptly answered.

"Sage, what's going—"

"Wesley, Sherry Yates isn't the next target. It's a writer named Julia Rose."

"What? How do you—"

"I don't have time to explain." She paused, emotion welling up inside her. She needed support on this one. She needed him to at least believe her. "Wes," she said, "I need you to trust me on this one."

A long stretch of silence made Taylor's mouth go dry, until finally, Wesley said, "Sage, you're a damn good agent, but I've gotta trust my own gut too. I'm staying here. You do what you need to do—get that other target in protective custody and call me if anything comes up."

Taylor let out a breath of relief, grateful he was at least supporting her. She admired and respected the fact that Wesley had to trust his own gut. Maybe he was right, and she was chasing her tail—but the stakes were too high to risk it. Taylor had to keep going.

"Thanks, Wesley," she said into the phone. "Stay safe."

Taylor hung up and pressed her foot on the gas. Everything felt like it was riding on this moment. If she was wrong, then it was more wasted time… but if she was right, then she would save a young woman's life.

Her heart thudded wildly as she reached Julia's street. It was a quiet suburb with houses nestled among trees. White picket fences and manicured lawns. The way normal life was supposed to be. From Taylor's experience, these clean-cut neighborhoods often harbored the darkest secrets.

She drove past Julia's house, number 27. The garage door was closed. Taylor eased her car a little closer and parked. She jumped out and approached the house. Her pulse pounded faster as she drew closer and rang the doorbell.

"Julia, it's Taylor Sage with the FBI. Please open the door."

No answer.

Taylor went to knock on the door—but it gently pushed open.

Taylor's stomach bottomed out, and she pulled out her gun. She didn't have time to waste.

The killer could be in here. He could already have Julia.

She took only a moment to send Wesley an SOS text before she pulled herself together. She was stronger than this. She had to be.

Slowly, she crept through the door. The living room was empty. She kept the gun up and moved forward.

"Julia, are you here? Are you okay?"

No answer.

Taylor's gaze shot from room to room as she made her way through the house. She tried not to let herself think about what the killer might have already done or about who he might have already killed.

Through the house, room after room. All were empty. Taylor began to doubt herself. Maybe Julia had just forgotten to lock the door.

But then she reached the kitchen—where a bowl of cereal had been knocked on the floor, milk and Cheerios all over the linoleum.

Taylor sucked in a sharp breath. *Shit.* The killer—he had to be here.

That was when she noticed the basement door, wide open.

And a light was on downstairs.

It was just a small light, but it flickered in the dark. Julia had to be down there, alone. With a killer.

Taylor swallowed her fear—just the way she'd been trained. This was where she had to be strong. This was her job, and she'd damn well do it right. She stepped toward the basement door, cringing at every creak of the wood.

"Julia?" she called out.

No answer.

She stepped down, her gun up and at the ready.

"FBI, Julia."

Taylor approached the staircase that led down to the basement. Slowly, she began to descend. Each step echoed through the empty space, the ringing noise amplified by the cold, concrete walls.

When she reached the bottom, she aimed her gun forward.

Then, a sudden sharp pain to the back of her head. Taylor's head became featherlight. A ringing in her ears. A heaviness in her body.

She fell to the floor.

The last thing Taylor saw before she lost consciousness was a woman tied to a chair.

***

When Taylor awoke, she couldn't move. She was tied to a chair—right next to Julia Rose, whose mouth was taped over with duct tape. The girl looked at Taylor with terrified brown eyes, and Taylor was quick to tune back into the situation.

She'd been fucking caught.

Unlike Julia, her mouth wasn't taped shut. "Julia, it's gonna be okay," Taylor said, fighting against her restraints. "I'm with the FBI. I'm going to get you out of here."

Julia just made noises beneath her tape.

"I wouldn't be so sure about that," a voice said.

Chills slithered up Taylor's spine, and she went still.

A man stepped out of the shadows. He was tall. Taller than Taylor, with a lean build, and he wore a black mask over his face. He was dressed all in black, with a black hat, black gloves on his hands, and a zipper running down the front of his outfit.

He walked toward her. As he spoke, Taylor could see his lips move beneath the fabric of his ski mask.

"Welcome back to the land of the living, Special Agent Sage."

She struggled against the ropes, but they were far too tight. He must have found her name from her badge. Taylor's teeth clenched in anger as she realized she was powerless to stop this. Julia flinched as the man strode up to her, and rage filled Taylor as he reached his hand toward her. She could do nothing to stop him. Taylor fought the ropes, trying to get out of the chair. She tried to kick the man, but he backhanded her. The blow sent a shock of pain through her head, but she didn't stop.

She had to get to Julia. She had to save her.

But it was no use.

His hand reached toward Julia--but all he did was rip the tape off Julia's mouth.

Julia was crying. "Please, don't kill me. Please!"

"Go ahead, beg," the man said.

"I won't tell anyone. I'll keep writing, and nobody will know."

"The hell you will," the man said. "You'll never write again."

Julia began to cry harder, and Taylor seethed with anger. "Why are you doing this?"

"I want you to know why you're dying," the man said. "This won't stop with you and Julia. I can't be stopped. Not until they see..."

He pulled back his hand and slammed it into Julia's face.

Taylor screamed and struggled against the ropes. She had to get to Julia. She had to save her.

The man looked at her, a smile in his eyes. "You think that was bad?"

Then, a sickening pop. Julia's nose, right on the bridge.

Taylor's stomach rolled.

"I'm the cure," the man said, his voice cold and clinical. "You're going to die here tonight. Then, tomorrow, a new story comes out. And as soon as I make my move, the entire world will finally see."

Taylor narrowed her eyes. "What the hell are you talking about?"

"I'm the cure," he said. "And there's no stopping it now."

She stared at him with wide eyes, trying to process his words. Who was he? What was he talking about? Whoever he was—he definitely fit the image she'd been building up of him.

As he leaned in closer, Taylor saw nothing but the eyes of a madman.

"Who are you really?" she demanded through gritted teeth.

He stared down at them for a long moment. Taylor could almost see the gears turning in his head as he decided how to reveal his identity. "I'm the only real one in this godforsaken town. Everyone is a fake. This bitch right here. And you, too." He pointed a finger at Taylor. "You think you're so much better than everyone else. You think you're so fantastic. You're nothing. You're the worst of them all."

He pulled a red ribbon from his pocket.

Taylor's stomach dropped to the floor.

There it was. The murder weapon.

He dove at a whimpering Julia. Taylor had to stop him. She had to keep him talking—he was clearly delusional, and she could use that to her advantage. She just had to stoke his ego, keep him talking about himself.

"What makes you so special?" she asked, trying to keep her voice steady.

He sneered at her. "I'm not the one who's special. I'm the only real one. I'm the only one who can see that this town is fake. All of it. Everything. Everyone." He paused. "This is all just a big, stupid game. A game you people think is real. But it's not. It's a game, and nobody here is what they seem. You are no different. The FBI... what a joke." His finger moved, pointing to his own chest. "I'm the only real one here, and everyone will realize that. I'll make them. And none of you will stop me."

Taylor had no words for how delusional this man was. It sickened her. At the same time, she had no idea how to stop him. The sense of powerlessness was enough to drive her mad, madder than him.

"But don't worry, Special Agent Sage," he said. Beneath his mask, Taylor could see he was smiling. "You'll get your turn. But I'm taking care of Julia first."

He dove right at her with the ribbon.

CHAPTER TWENTY EIGHT

As soon as the killer dove at Julia, Taylor knew she had to act fast. She flipped through the psychology textbooks in her mind, tried to think of what her father would do. What was the best way to keep someone like him distracted? She had to think fast, to say something that would keep him talking. *Just keep stoking his ego.* That had to buy them time.

"You're right," Taylor said. "You're not like the others. You're different."

When he stepped back, eyes trained on her, she let out a breath of relief. It was working—for now.

"I am different," he said. "I'm real."

Think, Sage. Stall him. Keep him talking.

"Why don't you show me your face?" Taylor asked. "I bet it's beautiful. You're real, right? So you don't need plastic surgery, or anything like that, to be beautiful."

"Hmm..." He once again smiled beneath his mask. "I suppose I could give you a small treat before I kill you."

Slowly, he peeled off the mask.

His face shocked Taylor. He was handsome, young, and clean-cut. He looked like he could be the face of a family-friendly breakfast cereal. If Taylor had to guess, based on appearance alone—he grew up rich. Which would explain why he'd left the Rolex without a care on Derek White.

But those eyes—they held so much rage. It chilled her to the bone. She had to keep him going—don't stop now. Maybe it was time to switch gears, get under his skin. If Wesley got her SOS text, then that would mean he should be there any minute. Taylor prayed that was the case.

"I'm different, too," she said.

He paused. "You are? How?"

"I know things. Secrets. Secrets that everyone in this town doesn't want me to know."

"What do you mean?" he asked, squinting. Taylor couldn't tell if he was buying it or not. But she thought back to the profile she'd built with her dad; about how it seemed likely the killer had some sort of paternal complex. So, Taylor took a guess:

"I know about you," Taylor said. "I know about your father."

The man froze. "My father? How could you possibly know about him?"

"He didn't love you enough, did he?" she egged on. "I bet he was a real fake."

A flash of rage crossed his eyes. He clenched his fists. "He was nothing. He was a failure."

"He was a fake," Taylor said. "He never loved you enough."

He was breathing heavier. The man's face twisted in anger. "He was a fake. He never loved me. He only cared about his stupid company. He didn't love anyone but himself."

That was the opening Taylor needed to really get into his head. "People like you and me—we're different. We're the only real ones in this town. I know things about you, too. I know how you were treated."

The man's face was red, angry, but he was listening.

Taylor continued, "I know you didn't fit in. You never will. You tried to make friends, but you were never good enough. You never were. And you love it. The fact that you're different. You're special. Nobody can treat you like your father did. Not now. Not anymore."

The man's face twisted in fury. Taylor had never seen a face like that. His eyes were so full of rage, and he stared at her with an intensity that made her skin crawl.

"Don't talk about my father." His voice was low. "You don't know anything about him."

"Oh, I know a lot about him," Taylor pressed. "I know he was a fake. All the money in the world, and he couldn't even be bothered to care about his own son."

"Idiot," he seethed. "You think I'm too stupid to see your little game here? You're just telling me what I want to hear."

Taylor opened her mouth to retort—to throw something else to keep him distracted—but he dove at her with the ribbon.

But this time, Taylor was prepared. She'd been through special training for this exact situation.

She waited until just the right moment. As soon as he was close, Taylor stood up, the chair still attached to her. She spun around and knocked the killer back, using the chair strapped to her back as a weapon. He fell to the concrete floor. Beside her, Julia screamed.

Taylor needed to get herself untied from this chair before he regained balance. This was it—the moment everything had been building up to. It was her chance to end this. Taylor strained against the

133

ropes, feeling them give—it wasn't much, but it was enough to free her hands. Taylor stood up, ready to face him.

But it was too late.

The man was on his feet, and he wrapped the red ribbon around Taylor's neck. She couldn't move. She couldn't breathe. She couldn't speak. Every time she opened her mouth to scream, the ribbon tightened against her skin, her windpipe closed, and silence filled the room.

"You're right," he whispered. "We're different. We're special. We're the only ones who can see the truth."

Taylor's vision began to go white as the circulation was cut off from her brain. Breathless, she tried to claw at the ribbon, but it was no good. She couldn't breathe; she couldn't break free.

"I liked you," he said. "I really did. I wish I could have let you join me. But you never knew how to listen."

The white faded as her vision closed in, until she could see nothing at all.

Suddenly, a loud noise.

The ribbon loosened, and Taylor gasped for air.

And then, Taylor saw him.

Wesley's dark hair. His gray eyes.

Taylor couldn't believe it. He'd found her. Wesley had found her.

"Stop and put your hands up!"

The man's hand loosened. Taylor pulled the ribbon off her neck and gasped for air. She looked over to see Wesley standing outside the room, gun out and pointed right at the man. If he made any movement, he would shoot him.

"You're done," Wesley said. "Drop your weapon, put your hands up--now!"

The man hesitated but didn't move.

"Do it!" Wesley said.

But the killer wasn't done. He ducked down, and Wesley shot. The sound echoed in the small room, piercing Taylor's ears. It had pegged the killer in the shoulder--but the killer went straight for him.

It was then that Taylor noticed the killer had taken her gun--and holstered it to the back of his belt.

Everything moved in slow motion.

"Wesley, look out!" Taylor screamed as the killer took the gun out.

Wesley's eyes widened, and he fired.

The killer's mouth opened, but no sounds came out. He turned and fired at Wesley. Taylor's eyes widened in horror as a bullet pierced

Wesley's shoulder. She had to move quickly. She had to help. She dove at the killer from behind and tackled him. She was not about to let her partner die.

The two of them fell to the ground, and the gun flew out of the killer's hand.

But then he was on top of her. The man wrapped his hand around her throat, and Taylor gasped. His hand tightened, and then loosened, but then tightened again. Taylor thought her eyes might bulge out of her head. But she couldn't move. She couldn't breathe. She could only fight. Her fingers clawed at the man's hand, trying to get him off her. But his hands were stronger.

The haze closed in, and Taylor struggled to pull in a breath. Her eyes fluttered as everything began to go black.

Suddenly, there was a noise. A loud bang. The killer's hand loosened, and Taylor gasped, sucking in air. She looked over to see Wesley's gun, lying on the floor next to them. Wesley was collapsed against the wall, clutching his shoulder. The man on top of her looked at Wesley.

Wesley had pegged him in the shoulder. Blood oozed from the wound and dripped down on Taylor.

"You can't shoot me," he hissed. "You can't kill me. Because I'm the only one who can see the truth."

He went to grab the gun again. In Taylor's mind, everything was moving fast-forward. Time was running out. It was up to her to bring this man in. She had to bring him down. She kicked him in the face and heard the crack of his nose. He fell back, and she dove for her gun, holding it right at him. Wesley, holding his bleeding arm, came up beside her.

The killer had run out of energy. He lay on the floor, a pool of blood forming around his shoulder wound.

"You can't kill me," he said. "I'm the only one who can see the truth."

"That's where you're wrong," Taylor replied.

Taylor pulled out the handcuffs and snapped them on him.

He struggled and protested, but she wasn't having any of it. She'd been through too much to stop now.

"You're in handcuffs," Taylor said. "You have nowhere to go, and there's no way you're getting away. How about...you start by telling me your name."

He glared at her with those brown, angry eyes, but said nothing.

"Why don't you tell me your real name," she said.

"My real name?" He smiled manically, blood streaming down his face, even as Taylor clapped the handcuffs on him. "Wouldn't you like to know," he taunted. "It really is a shame. I wanted to show you. I wanted to tell you. I wanted you to be a part of something new. Something special. I wanted to take you away. To the place where we were the only two people awake. I wanted to tell you all of the secrets."

"Shut up, shitbag," Wesley said.

Taylor pulled the killer to his feet, and now his head was hanging low as he laughed and laughed and laughed.

On the other side of the room, Julia Rose was still trembling in her chair—in all the chaos, Taylor had nearly forgotten about her. She handed the killer off to Wesley, then went to untie Julia.

"Help me," Julia pleaded, clearly still in shock. She'd been quietly whimpering.

"I've got you," Taylor said. She undid Julia's restraints, and the woman fell out of the chair.

She wrapped her arms around Taylor's neck.

"Thank you," she said. "Thank you, thank you, thank you. You saved me."

"It's okay, it's over," Taylor said, stroking her hair. "You're safe now."

As Julia burst into tears, Taylor took one last glance at the killer as Wesley dragged him toward the stairs.

Taylor hoped he was done. But the killer had one more thing to say to her, and it made Taylor's blood run cold.

"You're a faker, Special Agent Sage," he said. "One day, the whole world will know."

She clenched her teeth as he was dragged upstairs.

CHAPTER TWENTY NINE

Taylor sat in the briefing room at Quantico, listening to the silence. It had been hours since she'd been rescued, since she'd seen Wesley. The silence was almost louder than the gunshots. This was her own personal hell.

She'd lived through so much, seen so many things. She'd won. And yet she still felt so hollow. She sat there alone, waiting for more updates, trying not to think about the empty home she would return to later.

At long last, the door opened. Chief Winchester and Wesley walked in.

"Sorry for the wait, Sage," Winchester said. "Your partner here needed some stitches on that gunshot wound."

Taylor stood, observing Wesley, who was wearing a black T-shirt with a huge bandage wrapped around his shoulder. "How you feeling?"

"I'll live," he said. "I've had worse."

"You two are cute," Winchester cut in. "Let's debrief real quick, then you two can chat as much as you'd like."

"I need to start by saying…" Winchester paused. "Damn, this is not easy for me, but…well, it's been an honor working with you, Agent Sage. After everything you did here--you really are one of the best."

"Thank you." Taylor's eyes began to burn. She couldn't remember the last time someone had said something so nice to her.

"You've inspired me," Winchester said. "I'm proud to call you my agent."

"It's an honor to work with you, Chief," she said. "I really appreciate it."

"And you, Wesley—" Winchester's eyes fell on him. "You and Sage make a good team."

Wesley paused, wiping his hand on his jeans. "Yeah," he said. "I think we do."

"Now, onto the case," Winchester said. "The killer has been identified as Dylan Graham, a twenty-seven-year-old trust-fund kid who resented his wealthy parents for not spending more time with him. He was enrolled at Harvard, and during his time there, he started a blog that became incredibly popular with students. It was called 'The Real

137

Harvard.' He promoted himself as a truth-teller, who could expose all the people who were faking it in school. But his grades were crap, and his parents stopped paying for his tuition, so he had to move back here."

So, everything he'd done had been a statement against his parents.

He'd killed because he hated them for not supporting him. He'd threatened to murder, to bring down the all the fakes, all because he was mad at his parents and the way they'd raised him. He'd taken the lives of others because he couldn't stand his own.

Taylor shuddered. She was glad he was off the streets.

"Anyway, I'm glad I paired you two up," Winchester said. "You both deserve the rest of the day off, and Sage, I won't hear any buts on that. Go relax at home, okay?"

With that, Winchester left the briefing room. Taylor awkwardly faced Wesley. As tall and domineering as he was, over the past few days, Taylor felt like they worked good as a team. She appreciated that, although Wesley stuck to his own instincts and stayed at Sherry's house, he still encouraged Taylor to trust her own.

But then Wesley said: "Hey Sage, I owe you an apology."

Taylor blinked. "For what?"

"For doubting your instincts before."

Shaking her head, Taylor laughed. "That's funny, because I was just thinking about how much I respected you for trusting your own."

Wesley smiled and then he laughed, too. "Well," he said, "good partners."

"Good partners," Taylor agreed

Taylor smiled. "How's your wound?"

Wesley half-shrugged. "Barely a scratch."

"I don't know if I'd call a bullet wound a scratch," she said.

"I'll be fine. You know what the deal is with me."

Taylor nodded. Wesley was a tough nut. And even though she was glad he was okay, she didn't think he should try to seem indestructible.

"Good." Taylor paused. "I'm glad you're okay, Wesley."

"Thanks to you."

A silence fell between them, and Taylor knew it was time for her to head back. She dreaded that empty house, but at the same time, her eyes were starting to burn from the lack of sleep. Taylor left the briefing room and headed out of HQ. She made sure she wore her sunglasses as she walked through the parking lot.

Taylor got into her car and buckled up her seatbelt, letting out a sigh. It was over. Things were going to be okay. She popped her keys in the ignition and quickly checked her phone, and that was when she saw it.

A missed call from Ben,

Taylor's mind raced. Ben had called her? He'd been more or less ignoring her for days. And after the other day, when Taylor told him to go fuck himself... she didn't expect him to reach out again. She figured she'd have to go to him with some apology. If she still even wanted to make it work.

Part of her did, even after everything he'd done, mostly because Taylor was a fighter, not a quitter. She didn't just walk away from the people she loved. Even if, in this case, maybe it was time to throw in the towel.

Ben had treated her poorly. But if he was calling to make amends, she was willing to listen.

Taylor put in his number and called him back, a ball of anxiety buzzing in her chest. After a few rings, he picked up.

"Hello?"

"Hey," she said. "You called me. How are you?"

"Taylor..." His voice was deep and raspy. "I've been trying to get a hold of you."

"Oh, sorry, I didn't check my phone until now," she said, trying to keep her voice steady and calm. "What's going on?"

A pause on the other end made her heart thud in her chest. This didn't sound like it was leading into an apology.

"I'm sorry, Taylor," Ben said. "But... I've contacted a divorce lawyer."

There was a crackle in the line. Her grip tightened on the steering wheel.

"I'm sorry... what?" Taylor asked.

"I've contacted a divorce lawyer," Ben said. "I want to end our marriage."

Taylor's blood ran cold. She couldn't believe what she was hearing. Divorce? The word rang in her ears. Echoed all around her. She'd known this was a possibility, but hearing Ben say it made this whole nightmare so *real*.

In fact, it made the last several years of her life feel like such a waste.

Taylor was in her thirties now, not her teens or twenties. Time was everything, and she'd chosen to spend her time with Ben. Never in a million years had Taylor thought on their wedding day that it could end up like this.

"I'm sorry," Ben said. "I tried everything. I tried to make it work. I tried to fix it. But I can't. I... I just can't. You know why I can't."

What?

That was it? No *I'm sorry, honey, I messed up, let's make it work*? From the man who'd vowed to love her till death do us part?

No. No. No.

Taylor didn't say anything, her eyes wide and her mouth gaping.

Tears sprang to Taylor's eyes. She blinked them away. She wanted to scream, to say she didn't want a divorce, but she didn't say any of that.

Because in her heart, she knew it was the right thing to do.

Just because she'd spent so much time with Ben didn't mean he owed her forever. It didn't mean anything. They were just two people who'd been married for a while, and now they'd be divorced.

Ben would move on.

But so would she.

"Taylor?" Ben said. "Are you there?"

"Yeah," Taylor choked out, getting a hold of herself. "Yeah, I'm here."

"Are you going to cooperate?"

As much as it hurt, she was done begging for him. A cold sensation locked around her. If Ben wanted a divorce, a divorce was what he would get.

"Yes," she answered. "I'll cooperate."

"Good," he said. "I think this is the best thing for both of us."

"Yeah." Taylor blinked back tears. Her heart was still thudding in her chest.

"I'll be in touch," he said. "I'm sorry, Taylor. I'm sorry it didn't work out."

"Yeah," she replied, taking a shaky breath. "Me too."

"Bye—"

"Bye," she said, cutting him off and hanging up the phone. She dropped the phone in her lap, holding her breath.

All she could think about was how it was done. He'd done it, he'd gone and filed for divorce. He'd given up on their marriage. The happy memories forced themselves into her brain, as much as she tried to stop them, and alone in her car, Taylor broke down.

She didn't know what to do now. Her whole life had been flipped upside-down.

And yet, the one thing that had been with her through the toughest times was her training. Her training took over.

Her initial reaction was to break down. But she knew that wasn't going to help anything. She had to stay calm. She had to be in control.

Because now, nothing was going to be the same. But that was okay.

Knowing it was over, and having that closure, was more empowering than Taylor had realized it would be. It was time to take action. The coiled tension released from her body. She would keep fighting. She would keep fighting, she would keep training, she would keep moving forward.

If not for herself, for Angie.

EPILOGUE

At home in her bed—the bed she once shared with Ben—Taylor tossed and turned. She couldn't sleep. Every part of this house felt haunted now. Haunted by her marriage to Ben. Haunted by the memory of him leaving her.

He would come here once more, one day, while she was at work, and take all of his stuff. She'd come home to find all his stuff gone. Taylor had always found Ben's tendency to hoard annoying; she was a meticulous organizer, while Ben was more chaotic. But the thought of their bookshelves becoming bare, his architecture textbooks being gone, the spot on the shelf for his board games being empty—it all haunted her.

How was she supposed to keep living in this house with the ghost of their marriage? It was one thing for it to be over—Taylor had accepted that, but she didn't want to keep living here and being reminded of it. That was just masochistic.

Taylor couldn't stand being in bed. Being alone with her thoughts. So she got up and went to her car. It was late afternoon-now, and the September sun was hot. Taylor began driving aimlessly through town.

She didn't know where she was going, but she didn't care. She just wanted to keep driving. Drive until she was numb.

Eventually, she found herself in a parking lot by the boardwalk downtown. She got out and sat on the dock, in a secluded area devoid of tourists and travelers. She dipped her feet in the cool ocean and stared at the blue-gray foam that formed around her ankles. She thought of Ben, of how they'd gone to the beach once in a while when they were together back in Portland. How he'd splashed her, and how she'd splashed him back.

How he'd said how he couldn't wait for them to have kids so they could play in the water together.

Had they never loved each other? Or had they loved each other too much?

Taylor didn't know the answer. She didn't know the answer to anything anymore. She hated feeling like she was treading water. She hated feeling like she was lost, like she was at the bottom of the ocean, grasping for something, anything, to bring her back to land.

But there were no answers here.

And so, Taylor stood up, let her feet dry off under the sun, and changed direction to head downtown. She walked up the downtown strip, right toward the one place that had given her answers: Miriam Belasco's shop.

It was prime customer hour, but when Taylor went inside, Belasco was alone behind the front desk. She peered up at Taylor like she'd been expecting her.

"Ah, hello, Mrs. Sage," she said, her voice sultry and smooth. "You're here early."

"It's Ms. Sage now, please," Taylor said. "My husband is divorcing me." She scoffed, shook her head. "Maybe you already knew."

Belasco's long-lashed eyes softened. "I didn't know. I'm sorry."

A moment of silence passed, until Taylor said, "I don't know what I'm looking for anymore. I know I've asked a lot from you, and if you say no, I understand. Things with Ben are over for good now—I've accepted that. But... I can't shake this feeling that my sister is out there somewhere, and I'm missing something. Maybe... you could help me. One more time."

Belasco paused, observing Taylor with those all-knowing eyes. "Ms. Sage, I'm not a therapist; I can't help you with all your problems, and I can't tell you all you need to know. I'm merely a conduit. A pathway for information."

"I know that," Taylor said, trying not to be offended. "I'm not looking for therapy. And I know I need it, but right now, I just want answers." She pulled out her wallet and held it up. "I'll pay. You know I will."

Belasco always said she wasn't in it for the money, but Taylor would still pay her double, triple, or whatever she wanted, if it meant leading her even an inch closer to the truth about Angie.

"The money... has been helpful," Belasco eventually answered. "I do appreciate your business, Ms. Sage; I just want to make sure that coming here is still the best choice for you."

"It is," Taylor replied sharply. Even if that wasn't true.

"Okay," Belasco eventually said. "Come with me."

She led Taylor to the room in the back, where the table with the tarot cards waited for them. Taylor sat on one end, Belasco on the other. Taylor expected her to start shuffling the cards, but she didn't—instead, she peered at Taylor inquisitively.

"I'm not going to give you another reading today, Ms. Sage," Belasco said. "The other day, when I held your hands—the visions I got

143

were strong, some of the strongest I've ever received. I would like to try it again, if it's okay with you."

With bated breath, Taylor nodded.

"Give me your hands."

Sweating, Taylor did as she was told, and Belasco's smooth palms rested on hers. The last time Belasco did this, she'd given Taylor ominous details about Angie—and a phantom child in her future. Taylor hadn't given much merit to the latter, mostly because she didn't even have a husband to have a child with anymore.

The child was vague. But Angie—she seemed real. She could be real. The predictions, combined with Taylor's too-vivid nightmares about Angie... it had to mean something. It had to.

Taylor's stomach was clenched as Belasco shut her eyes.

Moments passed. Nothing happened, until—

The candles flickered.

Taylor looked around the room, alarmed. It seemed there was an energy in there—one she could feel, but not see.

Then, Belasco opened her eyes. But when she did, they were completely white, rolled back into her head.

Taylor pulled her hands back, afraid Belasco was having a seizure.

"Miriam, are you okay?" Taylor exclaimed.

But Belasco was holding out her hand now, creating a motion on the table—almost like she was writing. Taylor had no idea what to do.

"A... pen..." Belasco said.

Panicking, Taylor ran to the front desk and grabbed paper and pen. Belasco was still making the movement when Taylor returned. She placed the paper beneath Belasco's hand and positioned the pen in her fingers.

Belasco began to draw a symbol.

It was like a circle on top of a squiggle. No—the squiggle represented a *wave.*

But Taylor couldn't believe what she was seeing. This symbol—it was familiar.

She had seen it somewhere before. She was sure of it.

"Someone will be coming into your life soon," Belasco said, struggling to get the words out. "They will be from another place, another time."

"My sister?" said Taylor. Her heart beat wildly in her throat. "This doesn't make any sense."

"It will make sense to those who listen," said Belasco. "Someone is reaching out from across the ocean."

Taylor's eyes widened. She remembered the fortune teller was fond of riddles. She didn't have time to puzzle it out; she was still processing this new information.

Belasco's eyes began to return to normal. Just like that, the energy in the room was gone. Belasco let out a long breath, and then she collapsed. Taylor panicked, afraid she was going to be sick.

She didn't want to believe in supernatural forces anymore. She didn't want to believe that her sister—or whatever this was—was reaching out to her across the ocean. She didn't want to believe that she still had a sister to find.

But, oh God, she did.

Helpless, Taylor rushed to Belasco's side, afraid that the woman was hurt.

"Miriam?" She shook Belasco's shoulder.

Belasco wore a vague smile as she opened her eyes. "I am all right."

Taylor let out a breath of relief. "Thank God. What did all of that mean? I swear, I've seen that symbol before."

"I don't know what it means, Ms. Sage... but..." Belasco reached out and held Taylor's hand, gripping it tight. "You must find out. You must."

Taylor's jaw tightened, and she held Belasco's hand firmly. "I will," she vowed.

Belasco pulled her hand back and got to her feet.

She sat on the edge of the table and looked down at Taylor. Her expression was serene, but at the same time—tense. Taylor knew it was time to go. She didn't know if she believed the so-called visions, but she remembered what Belasco said: *Someone will arrive in your life soon.*

Someone will be coming into your life soon. They will be from another place, another time.

Someone. Not something.

Taylor paused before she went outside. She didn't feel like she was just leaving a psychic shop anymore. She felt like she was leaving a life preserver that might just keep her from drowning. She opened the door and stepped out into the sunlight, feeling lighter than she had since she moved to Pelican Beach. Taylor wasn't sure if it would be the last time that she'd see Belasco. But either way, for the first time since she'd come to this town... she was hopeful. She felt like she was moving in the right direction.

She had seen that symbol before.

Now, she had to find out *where.*

NOW AVAILABLE!

DON'T FLINCH
(A Taylor Sage FBI Suspense Thriller—Book 4)

A new serial killer is kidnapping women across the city, and his MO eerily matches with Taylor's own sister's disappearance. Could it be a coincidence? Or, after all these years, is Taylor about to find out if her sister's alive—and bring her home?

"Molly Black has written a taut thriller that will keep you on the edge of your seat… I absolutely loved this book and can't wait to read the next book in the series!"
—Reader review for Girl One: Murder

DON'T FLINCH is book #4 of a brand-new series by critically acclaimed and #1 bestselling mystery and suspense author Molly Black.

When the tarot reader gives Taylor a mysterious clue—a landmark from her childhood—Taylor races to put the pieces together, unearthing long-buried secrets along the way. Her determination to uncover a new lead upsets her family and vexes her partner—but Taylor knows that finding her sister is worth any price.

But is everything really as it seems?

Or is someone toying with her?

A page-turning and harrowing crime thriller featuring a brilliant and tortured FBI agent, the TAYLOR SAGE series is a riveting mystery, packed with non-stop action, suspense, twists and turns, revelations, and driven by a breakneck pace that will keep you flipping pages late into the night. Fans of Rachel Caine, Teresa Driscoll and Robert Dugoni are sure to fall in love.

Future books in the series will be available soon.

Molly Black

Bestselling author Molly Black is author of the MAYA GRAY FBI suspense thriller series, comprising nine books (and counting); of the RYLIE WOLF FBI suspense thriller series, comprising six books (and counting); of the TAYLOR SAGE FBI suspense thriller series, comprising six books (and counting); and of the KATIE WINTER FBI suspense thriller series, comprising nine books (and counting).

An avid reader and lifelong fan of the mystery and thriller genres, Molly loves to hear from you, so please feel free to visit www.mollyblackauthor.com to learn more and stay in touch.

BOOKS BY MOLLY BLACK

MAYA GRAY MYSTERY SERIES
GIRL ONE: MURDER (Book #1)
GIRL TWO: TAKEN (Book #2)
GIRL THREE: TRAPPED (Book #3)
GIRL FOUR: LURED (Book #4)
GIRL FIVE: BOUND (Book #5)
GIRL SIX: FORSAKEN (Book #6)
GIRL SEVEN: CRAVED (Book #7)
GIRL EIGHT: HUNTED (Book #8)
GIRL NINE: GONE (Book #9)

RYLIE WOLF FBI SUSPENSE THRILLER
FOUND YOU (Book #1)
CAUGHT YOU (Book #2)
SEE YOU (Book #3)
WANT YOU (Book #4)
TAKE YOU (Book #5)
DARE YOU (Book #6)

TAYLOR SAGE FBI SUSPENSE THRILLER
DON'T LOOK (Book #1)
DON'T BREATHE (Book #2)
DON'T RUN (Book #3)
DON'T FLINCH (Book #4)
DON'T REMEMBER (Book #5)
DON'T TELL (Book #6)

KATIE WINTER FBI SUSPENSE THRILLER
SAVE ME (Book #1)
REACH ME (Book #2)
HIDE ME (Book #3)
BELIEVE ME (Book #4)
HELP ME (Book #5)
FORGET ME (Book #6)
HOLD ME (Book #7)
PROTECT ME (Book #8)
REMEMBER ME (Book #9)